THE
LAST
RESORT

Emily Gallo

The author may be reached at ecegallo@gmail.com

www.emilygallo.com
http://emilygallo.blogspot.com/

ISBN: 9781950561117

Acknowledgments

Enormous gratitude to my stellar editors, Daniel Nauman and Chris Saur for always knowing the better way to say it.

Thanks also to my audio producer and cover creator, Glenn Tucker, who has tech savvy as only one of his many talents.

Thanks to my husband, David Gallo and my friend, Rafiki Webster, both of whom not only give me great advice, but also have to listen to me spew out my crazy ideas.

Thanks also to my assistant, Christopher Barboza, who has brought me to a whole other level of marketing and publicity.

And as always, I want to thank Tin Roof Café for providing me a place to write with my endless cups of Earl Grey tea.

THE FARM

1

GARBERVILLE IS A TOWN OF LESS THAN A THOUSAND THAT SWELLS IN THE FALL WITH AN ANNUAL MIGRATION OF YOUNG PEOPLE FROM ALL OVER THE WORLD. They are lured by the chance to make thousands of dollars manicuring the marijuana plants that have been cultivated surreptitiously in the forests, farms and hamlets for decades. The town sits right off the 101 freeway, two hundred miles north of San Francisco, in the lush Emerald Triangle, so named because it is the largest cannabis-growing area in the United States. There are so many pot farms that it has been said that everyone's livelihood is somehow dependent on the marijuana industry.

Dutch Bogart moved here in the early 1970s, bought an old homesteader's farm deep in the forest, and started growing long before it was legal. He grew up in southern California and had been writing songs and playing guitar from an early age. He played the coffee house circuit and graduated to clubs and music festivals. Local musicians who went on to become famous themselves started playing his songs and his course was set. His guitar style was southern blues, but his songwriting fell neatly into the more lucrative rock and roll category. Disillusioned and drained by the bright lights and groupie mentality, he decided he had enough money and recognition to focus solely on songwriting, with occasional gigs for kicks and inspiration.

He designed his house on Frank Lloyd Wright principles: large, low and angled with lots of redwood and glass. There was plenty of room for visiting musicians, a studio to jam and record in, and original art on the walls. He refurbished the barn into a dormitory for the trimmers and made it the best living situation for workers in the Emerald Triangle so they would keep coming back every harvest. He didn't want to have to hire and train new ones who proved incompetent or untrustworthy. This was the worst part of the business. The operation was well hidden from strangers by the old homesteader's apple and walnut trees and the surrounding forest of oak, madrone and fir.

Dutch stopped playing guitar and pushed back his long gray hair when he heard Juniper's car pull up. Harvest season was over and Juniper had been gone for the last few days, so it had been quiet on the farm. It was just Homer and a couple of trimmigrants from Quebec, who had asked to stay on for a few days because they hadn't decided where to travel next.

Dutch went outside to greet the arriving trio, giving Juniper a questioning look when he saw a young woman stumbling out of the car. She was so thin and frail that she could have been a child, but Juniper had already told him on the phone that she was in her mid-twenties. "This is Scarlett. She needs to rest, so I'll take her to my room for now until we figure out where to put her," Juniper said hastily. She put her arm around Scarlett's shoulder and guided her into the house.

Dutch turned to the old black man carrying a battered suitcase and a well-worn guitar case with Buster Fingerpickin' McCracken written across it and grinned. "It's a real pleasure to meet you, Buster," Dutch said as he reached for his hand to shake. "You've been a real inspiration to me and all my generation of blues guitarists."

"You ain't done too bad for yourself either, Dutch. I know your music."

"Are you hungry?" Dutch asked.

"I wouldn't mind a little something in my stomach."

"How about a beer or some weed?"

"Gotta lay off the alcohol. At least until I know I can handle it. Wouldn't mind a toke or two though."

"Come on in my music room." Buster followed Dutch and oohed and aahed over all the musical instruments, recording equipment, and music awards on the wall. Dutch went to the kitchen and came back with an assortment of crackers and cheese. He rolled the joint and passed it to Buster.

Buster took a long toke and shook his head. "You just never know what the lord has in store for you. You know, I can't give you much money —"

"I don't need any money," Dutch interrupted. "You've been an idol of mine since I was a teenager."

"You been living up here long?" Buster asked.

"Thirty-five years give or take."

"Growing all that time?"

"It's been very lucrative. I didn't always make a lot of money with my music."

Buster chuckled. "We don't get into that business to make money. You were smart." He looked around the room. "You got all this from selling pot?"

"That and some good luck. I ended up writing songs and playing in some bands that did very well in the seventies."

"That ain't all luck. As I said, you made some wise decisions. And I reckon you didn't let the weed seduce you."

"I saw too many of my friends and peers throw away their lives and careers. I stayed in control." Dutch grinned. Buster smiled at Dutch and nodded. He picked up his guitar case and opened it. Dutch got his guitar off its stand and started playing "Sweet Home Chicago." Buster joined in.

Scarlett stared at the ceiling of Juniper's room. "Are you coming to bed now too?" Scarlett called out.

"Not yet," Juniper answered from down the hall. She poked her head into the room. "I have some things to do first."

"I'm sorry," Scarlett whimpered.

Juniper came to her and kneeled on the floor. "All of this wouldn't have happened to you if I had kept in touch with you after I left."

"Oh, please, Juniper, don't say that."

Juniper sighed. "Let's talk more tomorrow. Okay?"

Scarlett sniffled and nodded. Juniper brushed her hand over Scarlett's hair, trying to imagine how awful her life must have been these last ten years. She didn't really want to hear about it, but she knew Scarlett needed to talk about it.

Buster and Dutch finished up a set of old blues numbers. "Did Juniper tell you where she found me?" Buster asked.

"Not really. Just that you'd hit on some bad times."

Buster cackled. "You could say that! My manager and record label screwed me big time. I get a small social security check and that covered rent in a crappy hotel in the Tenderloin. Anything more than that was from whatever I earned busking."

"Busking?" Dutch asked.

"I been spending my days playing in a BART station."

Dutch shook his head. "Man! How long have you been doing that?"

Buster shrugged. "Got a little too close to the bottle for a time, so I don't remember. Some years. Fucking manager took it all and the record company claimed I owed them, so I couldn't play any clubs or concerts. All the money I earned would have gone to them. You're saving my life letting me stay here. I'm too old to live like that."

"I'm glad Juniper found you."

"What's her story, anyway?"

"She didn't tell you on the drive up here?" Dutch asked.

"Not much. She only said that she hadn't been down to San Francisco for a long time."

"Yeah, she doesn't like being reminded of her crappy childhood in the city. She lived in foster homes until she was eighteen. She spent her twenties hitchhiking around the west coast and finally found trimming marijuana to be a lucrative seasonal job. The rural life agreed with her, so she ended up staying here. She bought a horse, and learned all aspects of the pot business and has become what they call a "trim mama."

Buster chuckled. "Trim mama?"

"She handles all the trimmers during harvest season. She also takes care of the house so I can focus on the growing and the business end."

"You're still doing music, ain't ya?"

"Here and there, an occasional gig. And I'm still writing songs for others."

"Juniper said there's a guy named Homer who lives here too. She said he's an old guy like me."

"Yeah, Homer's an old carney. Did electrical work for the circus too, so he's handy here when he can get around. He's got Parkinson's Disease."

"Oh man, that's awful shit. Like that actor guy Michael J something. Muhammad Ali had it too, didn't he?"

Dutch nodded. "Weed helps his tremors and so does listening to and playing music. Even dancing. It's pretty amazing."

"No kidding!"

"He's sleeping now. You'll meet him tomorrow."

"He don't need no nurse?"

"Juniper takes care of him, but he doesn't need much. A couple of kids from Canada who were trimming during harvest stayed on while Juniper was in San Francisco. They'll be leaving any day. They can't stay here more than six months on their visa."

"You got all those bedrooms?" Buster asked.

"The trimmers stay in a building out back. But there are enough bedrooms for you to have your own." Dutch stood. "Let me show you. Tomorrow we'll tour the farm."

2

EVERYONE HAD WANDERED INTO THE KITCHEN BY EIGHT THE NEXT MORNING. Introductions were made all around over steaming cups of coffee. Homer felt pretty well and he was thrilled to see Juniper again. They had become quite fond of each other, and he relied on her more than he acknowledged. Homer was interested in comparing notes on life on the road with Buster, and Buster thought Homer was quite a character. Scarlett, however, stayed in the background, smiling wanly when introduced, but obviously not up to conversation. The two Canadian trimmigrants joined them in the kitchen for breakfast. Dutch introduced them to the rest of the group. "This is Pierre and Camille. They're from Quebec. They'll help us in the fields with the post harvest cleanup before moving on."

After breakfast, Camille and Pierre followed instructions from Dutch and Homer and did the grunt work. They pulled out old plants and knocked the loose soil from the roots. Later they would add compost to the Smart Pots and plant vetch in the pots. Homer had advised Dutch that the vetch adds nitrogen and keeps the rain from compacting the soil. Buster proved not to have much stamina for "work a little too much like cotton pickin'" and proved better at admiring the surrounding scenery and mimicking the birds.

Besides the few acres devoted to planting the marijuana, some of the land was dedicated to fruit and nut orchards and vegetable gardens. There was a large pond, a couple of creeks bordered with alder trees, and fields of wildflowers. Much of the land was forested with large, mature trees such as oak, Douglas fir, pine and madrone, providing acres of land to ramble and lose oneself in.

Juniper and Scarlett stayed in the kitchen to clean up after breakfast. It was awkward at first, and they both scrubbed unnecessarily so they wouldn't have to talk. But finally they were done and Juniper poured herself another cup of coffee. "Do you want some coffee?" she asked Scarlett as they sat down at the kitchen table.

"No. My stomach is still kind of funky."

Juniper sighed. "What are you on?"

"I have no idea. Whatever he gave us to keep us placid and submissive."

"Dutch will have an idea what to give you to help you come off whatever it is."

"I'm sorry, Juniper." Scarlett started to cry again.

"Why do you keep saying you're sorry?" Juniper snapped back. "None of this is your fault."

"But you always encouraged me to be strong and stand up for myself."

"Don't blame yourself. We'll work on getting you on the right track."

"Why did you look for me after all these years?" Scarlett asked meekly. "I mean I'm not mad or anything that you didn't look sooner." She covered her face with her hands. "Oh, how could you have known?"

Juniper took Scarlett's hands into her own. "I just wanted to forget that part of my life, which meant I had to forget about you. It's a horrible thing, but true. Now I'm strong enough to look back . . ."

"You had every right to leave and not look back." Scarlett spoke to the ceiling. "Anyway, the foster home wasn't that bad."

"Not compared to what happened after you left," Juniper replied.

"It happens all the time. I turned eighteen and had nowhere to go. These men prey on young women who age out of the foster system. They find us and offer us a place to live and tell us they'll give us jobs." Scarlett sighed. "Only we didn't know what the jobs were."

Buster entered the kitchen noisily, panting and stomping mud off his shoes. "Damn this farm is big! Almost got myself lost finding my way back to the house!"

"Yeah, there's a lot of space," Juniper replied absently, dropping Scarlett's hands.

"I probably didn't even see most of it. You got a forest and pond and orchards? Jesus! Farms I grew up around in Mississippi didn't have all that." He laughed. "Course, I wasn't living near any plantation or nothing. We was just sharecroppers." He patted Scarlett on the shoulder. "You feeling better today, missy?"

"A little," she murmured, trying not to react to his touch.

"The worst is over," he said.

"Very true and you don't even know half of it," she answered with quiet dignity.

"I got an inkling. I've been on this earth way too long not to recognize it. Anyway, you're here now. That's the important thing. Now I'll just shut my old trap and go take a load off. Is lunch at any particular time?"

"You're on your own for lunch," Juniper answered. "I just do breakfast and dinner."

"Suits me. And thanks." He left the kitchen.

"I think I want to go back to bed too," Scarlett said as she started to follow him out.

"I'll check on you in a bit," Juniper said.

"Hey, you don't have to do that. I'm okay."

"It makes me feel better."

"Please stop feeling guilty."

"If I had kept tabs on you, you wouldn't have been sucked up by that sex ring. Plain and simple. I knew your birthday. I knew the day you turned eighteen and would have to face everything I had to face. But I was still running then, still searching for something far away from my past. So just let me mother you a little bit again, like when we were kids, okay?" Juniper wiped a tear from her eye and pulled Scarlett close. "You're safe now."

Scarlett started to cry. "I know," she said before running off to her room.

Juniper sat down at the kitchen table and buried her face in her hands, letting her tears flow. Dutch walked in with Homer and she grabbed a napkin and hurriedly blew her nose. "Allergies," was her stuffy, proffered excuse. Dutch raised a knowing, bushy eyebrow in response and gave her a soft knowing smile.

"Never knew you to have allergies," Homer said.

Juniper ignored him with, "How much clearing did you get done?"

"Most of it," Dutch answered. "Pierre and Camille want to go down to San Francisco for a few days before they catch a flight. I told them you or I could drive them into town."

"Well, they'd better get going. The bus leaves at noon."

Dutch looked at the clock on the stove. "I'll tell them. Do you mind driving them?"

"Sure. Homer, want to take a ride into town?"

"Not today, darling. I got some figuring to do on how we want to do the clones."

"Okay. Do you want anything?"

Homer laughed. "Only what you ain't gonna buy me!"

"Do you really want some chips and candy that badly?" Juniper sighed.

"Nah. I'll wait 'til I go to town." Homer winked at her. "Wouldn't want you to be seen buying that crap."

Dutch left to find the trimmigrants and Homer started out the door of the kitchen into the hall, but his gait grew wobbly and his hands started to tremble. "Is the pipe in your room full?" Juniper asked.

"Yeah, Dutch filled it for me earlier."

"Do you need help getting to your room?"

"I'll make it," he answered as he shuffled out.

Juniper grabbed a couple of hemp bags for groceries and went to an old pick-up truck to wait for the trimmigrants. Soon Dutch appeared with the Canadians while finishing a phone call. "That was a guy named Luther. I forgot to tell you that Jed called while you were away and asked if Luther could come stay at the farm for a while. Apparently he's at the Eel River Café. He arrived on the early bus from the city, but didn't want to call too early, so he's been walking around town. Can you pick him up?"

"The more the merrier, I guess," Juniper sighed as Pierre and Camille got into the truck, throwing their baggage in the back. "When do I get my Salvation Army uniform?"

"You'll have to settle for a merit badge for lifesaving," Dutch said loftily, slapping the fender of the truck.

Juniper started the engine and swung the truck around towards town.

LUTHER

3

It was August 1998 and Luther was waiting to start college in September. After dinner he went to the playground to join a pickup basketball game. There were several people playing, some of whom he had seen before, but no one he knew personally. When it got too dark to see, they asked if he wanted to join them for a beer. Luther didn't have a car, so a couple of them offered him a ride. They stopped at a convenience store to buy a case of beer. Luther stayed in the car while the other two went inside. Two shots rang out. One of the guys ran out the door and down the street. Luther ran inside and saw two people lying motionless on the floor. One was the driver of the car and the other was a middle-aged woman. Both of them had guns in their hands. Two teenage girls sat against a cooler, crying hysterically. And that's when Luther's life changed irrevocably. He never made it to college. In fact, he never made it home that night. In a matter of minutes he was sitting in the back of a patrol car charged with murder.

Luther was a tall, handsome, lanky African-American in his late thirties. He stood on the San Francisco corner and watched the bus drive off before walking tentatively into the café. He was tired of answering questions. He wasn't interested in a book deal or another lawsuit. He just wanted to get as far away as possible from the place he had lived for twenty years. He wanted to forget everyone connected with it. He wanted to bask in his exoneration and freedom. This wasn't even about a fresh start. It was about leaving behind the memories and the scars that had been etched into his mind and body. He had lied to his lawyer and the warden when he told them that he had a nephew who lived in San Francisco's Richmond District. That's where the bus dropped him off. But there was no nephew. He had been disowned and forgotten by his family other than his mother, and she had died several years ago. He had won the lawsuit and might get some money eventually, but now he had two hundred dollars and a plastic bag holding his few possessions.

He stopped at a café and read what was written on the chalkboard and was bewildered by the menu and shocked at the prices. After twenty years in San Quentin though, he knew there would be a lot to get used to. Chai? Café

Macchiato? What were they? "Do you have plain old coffee?" he asked the waif of a barista. She poured him a cup without responding. "How much?" he asked.

"Three dollars," she answered.

"Three dollars for a cup of coffee?"

She stared at him and sighed. "That's what I said."

Luther put three dollars on the counter and went to one of the tiny tables to contemplate his next move. He checked out the other customers. They were mostly singles, reading or working on laptops. A couple of them were talking to each other across the tables. As Luther sipped his coffee, he noticed several of them sprawled out as if they had been here a while and were not leaving anytime soon.

He glanced at the clock on the wall and saw it was after one. He threw his cup away and walked outside, took a left, and almost tripped over a homeless person asleep on the sidewalk. Luther muttered an apology to the seemingly unconscious woman and started walking east on Geary. He had studied the map and knew exactly where he was going. He took a right on Arguello, then a left on Anza, and looked up at the magnificent building at the top of Lorraine Court. The sign said "Neptune Society San Francisco Columbarium." He took a deep breath before walking through the door, and was greeted warmly by an older African-American man. "Hello, may I help you?"

"I'm looking for someone," Luther answered.

"What's the name of the person you're looking for?"

"Dorothy Banks."

"Follow me. My name is Jed."

"Luther." Jed took him to a computer terminal on a table. He punched a few keys and then said, "Here's the list. You can scroll down to find her." Luther looked at the computer screen but didn't move. "Could you just find it for me?"

"Sure." Jed sat down at the table and scrolled through as Luther watched him. "Here it is. Second floor. C'mon. I'll show you."

"Thanks." Luther followed Jed up the stairs.

"Let me know if I can help in any way. I'll be downstairs." Jed said as he walked away.

Luther stood in front of a glass door and took out the paper napkin he had taken from the café and wiped his eyes. "Hello Mama." He peered into the niche at a picture of an elderly Black woman next to a brass urn. There was a bouquet of artificial flowers in a sconce perched right outside the door. He stood silently for several minutes and then turned around and walked back downstairs.

"Is there anything else you need?" Jed called from behind as Luther started out the door. Luther turned around and looked into eyes that emanated compassion and integrity. Luther said nothing, only thought of the hard look and three dollar coffee he received earlier. He wavered, and Jed reached out and touched his elbow, leading him to a couple of chairs nearby. "How can I help?"

Luther sat silently, glancing up and around the large peaceful rotunda. He finally slowly shook his head in awe. "This is an incredible building."

Jed smiled. "I'd be happy to give you a tour and tell you some of the history, but something tells me that there's more on your mind."

Luther looked down at his lap. "I just got out of prison." He lifted his eyes and watched to see what Jed's reaction would be. His gut told him it would be a kind, welcoming smile, and he was right.

"When?"

"This morning."

"Is Dorothy your mother?"

Luther nodded. "I was exonerated, but she'll never know."

"She knows."

Luther looked away and wiped a tear off his cheek. "I hope so."

"How long were you in?"

"Twenty years."

"Twenty years? That's a long time." Jed put his hand on Luther's shoulder. "Do you have somewhere to go?"

"Nope. The rest of my family wasn't interested in having a convicted felon in their midst."

"Do you have any money?"

"Just the two hundred dollars they give everyone when they leave. The Innocence Project lawyers say there will be money coming, but they don't know how long it'll take."

"My wife works at Glide Church as a social worker. She can help you get set up with a place to sleep and some job prospects."

"You mean a homeless shelter?"

"Hey man, it's a bed."

Luther shook his head. "I just spent twenty years locked up, I'd rather sleep outside if I have to."

"I've been there. I get it."

Luther looked at Jed warily. "You've slept outside?"

Jed nodded and smiled. "I've slept outside in several cities. It takes some getting used to."

"I'll manage. My freedom will give me courage." Luther stood. "I'll figure it out."

"We open at nine tomorrow. You're welcome to wash up in the rest room."

"Thanks, Jed. It was nice meeting you." Luther started to leave and then turned around. "Are you here every day?"

"Just about," Jed answered.

Luther nodded and left. He had no idea where he was going. It was still early enough that the fog and chill hadn't descended on that part of the city. It may have been more than twenty years, but he hadn't forgotten how cold and damp it could be in San Francisco. Maybe sleeping outside wasn't a viable choice. If he went to a hotel, he would use up most of his two hundred dollars. He thought about calling Gordon, the Innocence Project lawyer who had helped get him out, but he was sick of all that. He sighed. Maybe he should talk to Jed's wife at Glide Church. If she was anything like her husband . . . He turned abruptly and went back to the columbarium. "Jed?" he called as he entered.

Jed appeared at the top of the stairs. "I'm up here."

Luther climbed the stairs. "I think I will go talk to your wife. What's her name and where's Glide?"

Jed smiled. "Her name is Monica and Glide is downtown in the Tenderloin. On Ellis and Taylor. Do you know where that is?"

"Not a clue. I lived in Oakland growing up. I didn't spend a lot of time here."

"Are you a walker? It'll take about an hour."

"Nothing I'd like better than to walk."

Jed smiled. "Go straight down Geary. When you get to Taylor hang a right. It's just a couple of blocks to Ellis."

"Thanks, Jed."

"Luther, I was in your shoes once. Not coming out of jail, but when I arrived in San Francisco I went to Glide for help. That's where I met Monica." He winked and smiled. "Maybe you'll meet the woman of your dreams there too."

"I don't know if I'm ready for that just now," he chuckled.

By the time Luther got to Glide Church, he was out of breath. He wasn't used to walking three miles. The hills of San Francisco were challenging. He walked in and looked around for a receptionist. A man carrying a large box of fruits and vegetables approached him. "You need some help?" he asked.

"Uh, yeah. I'm looking for Monica. She's a social worker here."

"Go on upstairs to the offices. Someone up there will find her for you."

"Thanks." Luther went up the stairs and entered an office. "I'm looking for Monica."

The woman looked up from a desk piled high with papers. "She's down the hall on the left."

Luther nodded and walked down the hall, peering into every office that had an open door. He came to a closed office with a sign on the door that said SOCIAL SERVICES. Luther knocked quietly.

"Yes?"

He opened the door tentatively and stuck his head in. "Are you Monica?"

"That's me. Come in, Luther. I've been expecting you." She stood and opened the door wider. "Jed called and told me you were coming." Monica was an attractive, mixed-race woman in her sixties whose engaging smile and welcoming eyes eased any apprehension Luther was feeling. She was the perfect archetype of a social worker. "Sit down." She pointed to a chair across her desk.

"Did Jed explain my situation?"

"Yes. He said you didn't want to sleep in the shelter. You'd have to wait on line to see if there's room anyway, and I can't do anything about that."

"What are my options?"

"Have you called the Innocence Project? Maybe there are some funds —"

"I don't want to talk to them now. I mean my lawyer has been incredible, but . . ." Luther trailed off.

" . . . But you're sick of it all. I hear it all the time and I get it, but it doesn't help you much in the long run. You have no family or friends you can stay with?"

He shrugged and shook his head. "Nope. I guess I'm feeling a bit overwhelmed. It all happened really fast. You'd think I'd have been prepared, but word came down yesterday afternoon and they released me this morning."

"So you are still listed as a felon, I guess. It takes a while for the powers that be to purge the records." Monica pursed her lips and looked through some papers on her desk. Luther watched her silently for a few minutes. "Oh, here it is," she finally said. "Wait here. I need to talk to someone." She got up and left her office. She came back after several minutes. "I got through to the owner of one of the hostels in town and they have space for you. You'll have to share a room and bath but it will only cost you twelve dollars a night."

Luther sighed. He didn't want to share a room with anyone, but anyone would be better than his cellmate was. Or dirty cold concrete. "Thanks."

Monica cocked her head and handed him a piece of paper with the address. "It's a start. I'll see if I can find some work for you if you want to stay in San Francisco."

"Let me think about it and let you know. I'm tired, confused, and hungry."

"We're serving dinner here in about an hour. The hostel is only a few blocks away. You could take a shower there and then come back here to eat. We can provide you with some clothes at our free store."

"Okay." Luther stood and started to leave.

"Oh, and Luther? Keep your situation to yourself. I pulled a few strings. They wouldn't have taken you if they'd known about your record." The reality of his situation hit home. It wasn't just about finding a place to sleep tonight. Luther shot her a defeated look, and she came around her desk to put an arm around his shoulders. "Things will work out, Luther," she said. "The system stinks, but with a little tweaking, doors start opening. Trust me."

"I guess I must," he said quietly, looking down at the worn floor. He gave her a sidelong glance. "I am grateful, Monica. Thank you."

She gave him a little shake. "Come back tomorrow morning and we'll work on the job situation next. Dinner is only served until six-thirty so make sure you get to the dining room before then."

Luther nodded and left. He decided to forego the free store until tomorrow and went to the hostel, hoping that his roommate wasn't there. He walked through the streets of the Tenderloin, glancing around at the people sleeping in doorways and huddled against buildings like it was trash day. There was no easy path to freedom.

4

THE HOSTEL WAS CERTAINLY A STEP UP FROM A JAIL CELL. There was a living room with a television, books lining the walls, a refrigerator and a microwave. It wasn't exactly homey, but it was quiet and felt safe. He paid the manager for four nights. That was fifty out of the two hundred, minus the three-dollar coffee. He would have liked to have his first real meal in a restaurant, but that was obviously not a luxury he could afford at this time. Luther climbed the stairs and walked down the narrow hall to room seven. He paused, knocked, and hearing no response, entered to find he was alone . . . at least for now. Neither twin bed appeared to be claimed, so he randomly lay down on one just to rest a little while. Silence fell over him like a warm blanket. He almost dozed off before realizing that he had to get back to Glide if he wanted to eat at all.

After dinner Luther returned to the hostel to find the living room bustling with lively, young people. He smiled politely as he squeezed through the group towards the stairway. He wasn't interested in socializing and hoped his room was still empty.

Luther opened the door and found a young man in his twenties with a trim beard and long hair pulled into a bun, sitting on the floor, reading a San Francisco guidebook. He wore headphones connected to an iPhone. He looked up at Luther and scrambled to his feet, pulling the headphones off his ears. "Bonsoir! Hello!" He reached his hand out to shake Luther's.

"Hi," Luther answered tentatively.

"Je m'appelle Jean-Paul. Et vous?"

Luther looked blankly. He knew he wasn't speaking Spanish, but he had never heard French spoken and wasn't sure whether that was the language. "Luther."

"Luther. Like Martin Luther King?"

"Uh, yeah."

"My English not good. You speak Francais?"

"Nope."

"Where you come?" Jean-Paul asked.

"You mean where am I from?"

Jean-Paul smiled sheepishly. "I learn still."

Luther pondered how to answer this. It was his first test. He heard Monica's warning repeat in his head. The fact of being born and raised in Oakland passed through his mind. "Northern California," he finally said.

"Oh bien, bien! You show me where I go!" Jean-Paul took out a guidebook and handed it to Luther.

This was not how Luther wanted to spend his first night of freedom. And besides, he had no idea. He was a teenager living in the ghetto when he was incarcerated. "I'm really not a good person to ask. Sorry."

Jean-Paul smiled and took the book back. "Okay. I try to make plan."

Luther nodded and went to the bed he used earlier. "Is this bed okay for me to use?"

"Oui, yes. I use other."

Luther lay down and closed his eyes. It was pretty early to be going to sleep, but he really didn't want to have any more conversation. If this was the only way to do it, pretend to be asleep, then that's what he'd do. Jean-Paul put his headphones back on and leafed through the guidebook while Luther lay back with his eyes closed, hoping that Monica would be able to find him a job and another place to live right away. It actually didn't take long for him to drift off. The long walk across town and all the emotions of the day caused him to sink into a deep sleep.

Luther got to Glide Church too late for breakfast so he went directly to Monica's office. She welcomed him in with a warm smile. "How did you sleep, Luther? I hope you had a nice roommate."

Luther laughed. "Well, he's nice, but he likes to talk. He's French and doesn't know much English. It wasn't easy. He asked me to give him ideas on places to visit. Not exactly my strong point, being a tour guide."

Monica laughed. "I looked at some of my job listings." She put her hand on his shoulder. "It's going to be hard until that felony conviction is off your record."

"I know."

"Did they tell you when your record would be wiped clean and when you'd get some compensation?"

Luther sighed. "Apparently it's a long process."

"I know," Monica frowned. "I was just hoping to hear something different for a change."

"It's complicated. I've learned not to expect much. There are a lot of things that *should* have happened to begin with . . ."

Monica nodded. "Well, let's see if we can't come up with a job where they will be sympathetic to your plight."

"Maybe San Francisco isn't the place to do that," he blurted out.

"Where would you go?"

"Maybe some place in the country."

"I know that sounds great, but there aren't the same level of services there that we have here. You'll be largely on your own with just two hundred dollars to your name."

"More like one forty-seven."

Monica sighed. "You know, I have a thought. Get over to the columbarium and tell Jed I said he should call Dutch."

"Dutch? That's his name?"

"Yes. He owns a farm up north."

"Okay. Thanks Monica."

She lifted crossed fingers. "It's our safest bet if you really want out of the city, unless something extraordinary crosses my desk."

"You're very kind."

"It's my job." She shrugged. "But I'll still take the compliment."

Luther started to walk toward the columbarium, but realized he was quite hungry. He knew there would probably be other places that served the homeless, but he didn't know where they were and didn't want to waste time. Up on the next block he saw the golden arches and he grinned. He hadn't had fast food in ages, and he was pretty sure he could get some sort of meal deal for not much more than yesterday's damn coffee.

When he finally arrived at the columbarium he found Jed setting up for a memorial service. "Hey Luther! How are you?

Come on over and give me a hand if you don't mind. People are going to start arriving soon."

Luther helped Jed set up the chairs in the main room and then swept up the anterooms while Jed got the flowers and an easel. A couple arrived and placed a large picture on the easel and a stack of memorial programs on a table. The room looked radiant by the time the rest of the mourners started arriving. The service was touching and Luther enjoyed being part of something that seemed real and significant.

It was after two when Luther and Jed finished tearing down the room and they were finally able to talk. "Monica said she was able to find you a room last night?" Jed said.

"Yeah, she's been a great help." Luther paused, trying to frame her request. "Hey, she told me to ask you about getting in touch with somebody named Dutch? That maybe he could help me find a place to live and a job?"

"Dutch? Do you want to go to Garberville?"

Luther shrugged. "I don't know. Where's that?"

"Humboldt County. A few hours north of here. Garberville is famous for its pot." Jed grinned. "Or infamous, depending on your point of view."

Luther chuckled. "And Dutch's farm?"

"Yep."

"Well, he shouldn't have a problem with my past then. Right?"

"You'd need to talk to him. Hey, are you hungry? There's a Szechuan restaurant really close. Otherwise there's a pizza place and a hamburger joint just a couple of blocks away."

"What's Szechuan?"

"Spicy Chinese."

"Never had it. It's been a long time since I had a good pizza. The stuff they called pizza at San Quentin was pretty bad. Maybe that?"

"Sure." Jed gave him money and directions. "What kind would you like? I can call ahead."

Luther smiled. "I don't know. I guess pepperoni?"

Jed nodded and Luther left, returning about forty-five minutes later with the pizza and a couple of sodas. They sat down in Jed's office and Luther gobbled down his pizza slice in what seemed like seconds. Jed laughed. "I guess you like pizza."

"You just can't imagine how much I miss real food."

"I can imagine. So how are the new digs?"

"You mean the hostel?" Luther shrugged. "Better than a jail cell. My roommate's a little annoying. He's from France and talks a lot."

"I called Dutch. He asked if you had any skills."

Luther shrugged. "No, but I can learn."

"You really want to go up there? His farm is in the middle of nowhere."

"Sounds exactly what I want right now. I'm finding the city a bit overwhelming."

"I get that."

"Well, Dutch wants you to call him."

"Okay. Can I borrow some change for a pay phone?"

Jed chuckled. "Dude, they don't exist anymore. Well, maybe in Garberville, but that won't do you any good here. We need to get you a cell phone. We can go after I close up here. The store should be open late."

They finished eating and then Jed handed Luther a caddy full of rags and glass cleaner. "Mind wiping the fingerprints off the niche doors for me?"

"Sure!" Luther worked steadily for almost two hours until he heard Jed calling him from downstairs.

Luther scrambled down the stairs to the front door where Jed stood, holding a rake and a hoe. "Yeah?" Luther said.

"I'd like you to do some weeding outside."

Luther looked at Jed warily. "Uh, I've never held a rake in my life. I grew up in the ghetto. We didn't exactly have yards and stuff. I don't know how to do that."

Jed laughed. "Well, you probably swept up some crap you spilled on the kitchen floor a few times before your mama found out and whooped you. Raking is pretty much the same motion, and one you better learn if you want to live on a farm. Let's go."

They went outside and Jed showed him how to rake the leaves and what were weeds and what were not and left him to fill a large plastic bag. When he came back, Luther had filled the bag and he held it out with a grin. "Nothing to whoop me over!"

"I ain't your mama anyway," Jed grinned. "Thanks, though." He glanced around. "Good job."

"Hey, you still have to talk to Dutch. It's not a done deal. Let's close up and get going."

They locked the door and the gate and strolled down Geary to a phone store. A sales person approached them immediately. "Need a new phone?"

"Not a new one," Jed corrected.

"Excuse me?"

"I don't have one." Luther explained.

"Oh!" The salesman's eyes brightened considerably at what he thought might be the chance to make commission on an expensive phone. "Let me show you the latest iPhone."

"He needs a cheap phone," Jed interrupted.

"You mean like a burner?"

"What's a burner?" Luther asked.

The salesman gave Jed an incredulous look and Jed leaned over to Luther and muttered, "Prepaid. Anonymous."

"An anonymous phone? Does that mean like unlisted?"

"Sort of," Jed sighed. He looked directly at the clerk. "How much will it cost him?"

"It depends how much you put on it," the salesman answered.

"Oh, like a phone card," Luther said.

The salesman gave Jed a sidelong glance before explaining. "Um, a burner is usually disposable. You throw it away after you use it."

"Why would I want to do that?"

The salesman laughed. "You really don't know this?"

Luther glared at the salesman. "No I really don't know this."

Jed frowned at the clerk and turned to Luther. "You can get a phone that you keep putting money on."

"How much is that?" Luther asked.

"It depends. Smartphones start at around fifty dollars."

"What's a smartphone?"

The clerk sighed heavily. "It's like a computer. You can use the Internet and get apps. How much do you want to spend?"

"Fifty total," Luther answered.

"I have a phone in the back you can have for twenty bucks. Then you can put sixty minutes on it for twenty bucks. All that plus tax would be less than fifty."

"Good."

The salesman went into the back of the store and within twenty minutes Luther had a phone and a very basic understanding of how to use it. He had made a step into the twenty-first century. "Let's see how you do adding contacts into your phone," Jed said as they walked out of the store. He gave Luther his number and watched him put it in the phone. "Okay, now here's Monica's and Dutch's." Luther put their numbers in and said goodbye to Jed. "Remember to plug your phone in when you get back to the hostel." Jed reminded him. "Call Dutch tomorrow morning."

Luther wagged his head. "Okay, Momma." Jed gave him a playful whack on the side of the head. "Thanks, man." Luther grinned. "I mean it."

Thankfully Jean-Paul wasn't in the room when Luther returned to the hostel. After plugging in his phone and playing with it for a while and learning a little more about how it worked, he lay back on his bed and contemplated what to do next. He could call the bus station to see how much a ticket to Garberville cost, but he didn't want to use up any of the sixty minutes on the phone. It was cheaper to walk to the station and ask. He decided to go downstairs and see if there were any interesting books or what might be on TV.

Jean-Paul was on a couch talking to a group of young men and women who looked just like him. "Luther! You come out with us tonight. We go to—" Jean-Paul turned to the group of people, "what you call again?"

"Pub Crawl," one member of the group answered.

Jean-Paul turned back to Luther and laughed. "Such funny name. Pub Crawl."

Luther had never heard of a Pub Crawl before, but he guessed that at least the beer would be plentiful and maybe even free depending on how drunk they got. He wouldn't mind getting a bit buzzed, just to forget everything. "What time are you going?"

Jean-Paul turned to the others and asked, "Bientot?"

"Let's go," one of them said as she went upstairs. The others followed to get their jackets.

Jean-Paul was a bundle of excitement. "I like so much these new friends."

"Yeah, they seem nice."

It was even better than he had expected. The group was from all over the world. They didn't care where anyone had come from and didn't ask. It was all about drinking and playing darts and pool. No one seemed to notice that Luther hadn't been paying for anything. It all got lost in the sharing of tabs and quarters on pool tables. The darts were free, as was watching sports on the huge TVs. Luther felt surprisingly comfortable, admiring the laid-back attitude of these travelers. By the time Jean-Paul and Luther got back to the room, they were drunk and exhausted. Both of them fell asleep in their clothes.

Luther slept too late to get to breakfast at Glide. In fact it was almost lunchtime when he started walking briskly toward the columbarium. Jed was busy giving a tour of the building when Luther got there, so he joined that group and heard the fascinating history of the building and some of the people whose remains were there. It was lunchtime and Jed gave him money to get some more pizza. "Have you called Dutch yet?" Jed asked when they had sat down to eat.

"I thought I'd wait until I was with you."

Jed nodded. "Okay."

"I was thinking how much it'll cost to get to Garberville," Luther mused.

"There's a bus. I've taken it," Jed replied.

"How much?"

"I think the fare was about fifty."

"I still have that much."

They finished eating. "Okay, Luther. Let's see you use your new phone."

Luther took out his phone and scrolled down to Dutch's name in the contacts. He pressed the number and put the phone to his ear, grinning at Jed. "It's ringing."

"See? You're a pro," Jed smiled back.

"Hello? Uh Dutch? This is Luther. Um, Jed talked to you about me?"

"How ya' doin'," Dutch answered matter-of-factly. "So I hear you want to come up to the farm?"

"Yeah."

"What can you do?"

"Um, what do you mean?"

"Do you know construction?"

"No, but I guess I can learn."

"So what kind of skills *do* you have?"

"Um, well . . . just that I'm eager to learn and will work hard." Luther looked at Jed who nodded and smiled.

"Okay. You can come up. I'm taking Jed's word on this so don't let him down. We'll see how you do."

"Oh thanks, man." Luther breathed a sigh of relief. "You won't be sorry."

"When will you be here?"

"I have to find out about the buses."

"Call me when you know." Dutch hung up.

"He said I can come," Luther told Jed excitedly.

"When do you want to go?"

"Right away. You think Monica could help me get back the money I paid for the nights at the hostel to help pay for the bus?"

"Probably. I think there's a pretty strong demand for those rooms. Let me see." Jed called Monica. "Looks good, Luther. Let's see when the bus leaves."

"I'll need to get my stuff at the hostel." And then he shrugged. "It's not like there's anything except some stuff I got from the free store at Glide. I don't really need them."

Jed gave him a look. "Well, you will need some clothes no matter where you are."

Luther laughed. "I guess you're right."

Jed called the bus station and found out the times. "There are two a day. One leaves in an hour. You won't make that one. The next is at 10 p.m. Trouble is it gets in at four in the morning. We can't ask Dutch to pick you up that early. I guess you could wait until tomorrow at two-thirty."

"I'd rather do the ten o'clock tonight and have the money back from the hostel. I can just wait for Dutch to pick me up. It'll give me a chance to look around the town."

"At four in the morning?" Luther shrugged again. "Up to you. Do you know where the bus station is?"

"I'll find it. Thank you Jed for all your help. And Monica too."

Jed lightly put a hand on his shoulder. "I have a favor to ask of you."

"Anything!"

"There's a friend of mine living there. His name is Homer. He has Parkinson's disease. He's a good guy. Tell him Monica and I will come visit him soon."

"Is he another person you helped by sending him to Dutch's farm?"

"Yeah."

"Then I look forward to seeing you at the farm." Luther hugged Jed. He sprinted off, finally feeling that he had a goal and a purpose.

Jean-Paul wasn't there when he got back to the hostel. Monica had called and he was able to get his money back. The proprietor asked for a forwarding address. He didn't know what to say so he just said Dutch's farm in Garberville and gave her his phone number. He scooped up his meager possessions and put them in the backpack and left. But he still had hours to kill before the bus left. And he would need to eat, even though he was still full from the pizza. He decided to have a last meal at Glide. Maybe

Monica was there now and he could thank her in person.

He also realized he needed to call his lawyer to give him his phone number. He dialed, having memorized the number from the many calls he had made from prison, but it went to voicemail. Doesn't anyone ever answer their phone? He left the message that he was going to work on a pot farm in Garberville and recited his phone number. He looked for Monica when he got to Glide, but she had left for the day. He ate dinner and excitedly set off for the bus station.

LEO/ TASHA

5

THE PLANE TOUCHED DOWN AFTER ELEVEN. It was three hours late, but in Las Vegas the night was still young. Leo, handsome, slightly built, white, mid-forties, stepped off the plane pulling a suitcase and carrying a battered canvas messenger bag over his shoulder. The conference would start the next morning at nine. He had time for a quick visit to the casinos for a drink and a couple of games, but he wanted to check in first. This year they were staying at the Luxor.

Leo was an organizer for the United Agricultural and Commercial Union. Their annual Retail/Trade Union conference was always held in Las Vegas. His local office was in Sacramento, but he was on the road most of the year. He was on his way to far northern California and he expected to be there for a while. Las Vegas would be an interesting diversion from what was ahead of him.

Leo checked into his hotel, and was on his way to the Bellagio by midnight. He wasn't much of a gambler, but he liked the clientele and he had befriended one of the dealers there. Every year he made a point of playing at her roulette table and they usually had a drink together after her shift. When he got to the Bellagio, he was happy to see that this year was no exception. He sat down and gave Tasha a slight nod. The dealers were not supposed to acknowledge any of the people at their table, so Leo would have to wait until after her shift.

Last year Tasha had opened up to Leo about her life. She had lived in Las Vegas for four years, gone to dealer school there and had been working at the Bellagio for three years. She had not told Leo anything about her past earlier than that. He also wasn't sure how old she was, but she looked to be in her late twenties or early thirties.

Leo lost about a hundred dollars at the table before Tasha was able to go on a break, a loss not to be taken lightly on his salary. As soon as her replacement sat down at the table, Leo scooped up what was left of his chips and followed Tasha as she walked away. "Hey, Tasha. Are you on a break or off for the night?"

Tasha smiled. "I'm off. How ya doin'," Leo? Is it that time of year again?"

"Yeah. Can we get a drink?"

"Sure, but not here. Where are you staying?"

Leo perked up. Did she want to come to his room? "Luxor."

"Oh, too far. Let's just go to Caesar's across the street." Leo's heart sank, but he followed her out. They settled into a booth and ordered a couple of drinks. "How long are you here for?" she asked.

"A few days. How have you been?"

Tasha sighed. "Been better."

"What's wrong?"

Tasha looked away. "I don't know. Maybe I'm just sick of the job."

"What would you like to do?" Leo asked.

"Get out of Vegas."

"That sounds easy enough. You must have money. Dealers make good wages."

"Some. Enough. It's just . . ." She looked away.

"What?" Leo asked.

She ignored his question. "So, what are you up to? You're always coming from somewhere and going somewhere. I don't even know where you live."

Leo laughed. "Sacramento. But I'm never there. You're right. I'm always on the road."

"Do all union organizers live like that?"

"No. It's my choice. I have no wife, no family, and no ties. And I like to travel."

"Yeah. I would too."

"And where are you from?" Leo asked.

"Illinois."

"Chicago?"

"I wish. No. Way down in the southern part of the state. Effingham."

"Quite different from Vegas," he joked.

"You think? It's not called Effing-ham for nothing."

Leo smiled. "Where would you like to go?"

"California I guess. That's where I was headed when I ended up here."

"So why did you stop here?"

"I met this guy who said that California was a really expensive place to live and that I could make a lot of money here dealing."

"I guess that was good advice. Where in California did you want to go?"

Tasha shrugged. "San Francisco or Los Angeles."

Leo smiled. "Well, you definitely picked the pricey places in California."

"They're the only places I knew."

"California's a big state. There are lots of places you could go. Sacramento got an influx of people from the Bay Area so it's gotten more expensive, but it's still cheaper than those cities."

Tasha straightened up. "So where else could I go?"

"Well, I'm going up to the northwest corner of the state when I leave here. The biggest city there is Eureka."

"I like the name. Are you going there?"

"Not exactly. Have you ever heard of the Emerald Triangle?"

"No. Sounds like something from the Wizard of Oz."

Leo burst out laughing. "Never thought of it that way!" he snorted. "The wizard, the flying monkeys . . . it's a trippy film alright."

"So it's called the Emerald Triangle because . . .?"

"I guess because it's really green and lush and a good place to grow pot. I'm going to work on getting the cannabis workers into the ACW."

"ACW?" Tasha asked.

"The Agricultural and Commercial Workers Union, where I work."

Tasha nodded. "So you're going to the farms?"

"Farmworkers, trimmers, dispensary workers . . . there are a lot of people that are ripe for organizing."

"How long will you be there?"

"I don't know. It should be easier in the marijuana industry. Even the owners are pretty liberal and supportive of unions."

"Did I ever tell you that I have a BA in Botany?"

Leo's eyes widened. "You have a college degree? In Botany?"

Tasha laughed. "There aren't any good jobs with just a bachelors. Anyway, I make much more money dealing at the casinos."

"Would you rather do something with plants?" Leo asked.

"That's what I was thinking."

"Like on a pot farm."

She shrugged, looked at her phone, and stood abruptly. "I need to go, Leo."

"Someone waiting for you?" he asked.

Tasha smiled but didn't answer. "Will I see you tomorrow?"

"I'll come by after the day's workshops. What time will you get off?"

"I'll try to get off early. Like about nine." She kissed him on the cheek before walking off.

Tasha got to the front door of her apartment and took out her key. Her client wasn't expected for another fifteen minutes so she would have time for a quick shower. She opened the door and saw the light on in the living room. She thought surely she hadn't left it on since she left for work during daylight hours. When she entered her bedroom she switched on the overhead light and saw two men standing by the window. "Hello Tasha." She turned toward the bed. A large man lay on the covers, fully clothed. His arms were folded behind his head and his legs were crossed.

"How did you get in?" Tasha snapped.

The man laughed loudly and looked at the two men standing by the window. "Can you believe that? She's wondering how we got in." The two men joined in the laughter. He turned back to Tasha. "I never have a problem breaking and entering, my dear."

Tasha took a deep breath. "Well get out. I'm expecting someone shortly."

"This doesn't have to take long. We'll take care of everything so you never have to make your own appointments. It'll make your life so much easier."

"I've told you a hundred times I'm not interested."

"Yes, I know you have. But it's time you realize you don't have a choice, Tasha."

"No! Now get out and leave me alone."

The large man looked at the two by the window and nodded. They grabbed her, pulled her onto the bed and held her down while the large man sneered at her. "I don't think you want to say no, Tasha."

"You can't intimidate me Preacher Boy! Get your fucking goons off me!"

"Ooh, you're making me mad now. You don't want to do that, does she boys?" They pulled her arms and legs away from her body, leaving her spread eagle. Preacher Boy punched her and ripped off her blouse. "Now, you sure you still don't want to work for me?"

Tasha squirmed, trying to get out of their grip. "Leave me alone!" she screamed as tears started to roll down her cheeks.

Preacher Boy yanked down her pants. "Nothing like a screaming woman to turn me on." He fumbled with his fly, pushed the crotch of her panties aside and climbed on top of her. The two men continued pulling at her extremities and watched as Preacher Boy raped the struggling, whimpering Tasha. In the middle of it, the doorbell rang several times. Then the knocking began followed by Tasha's phone ringing. Finally, Preacher Boy came and the ringing and pounding stopped. He rolled off her and zipped up. "Now you know, baby," Preacher boy sneered. "You don't have a choice."

"It's my body," she sobbed.

"Jesus, aren't you a stupid fucking bitch," he muttered. "Boys, show her whose body it is." The two men yanked her off the bed and started beating her, slapping her face and twisting her arms and legs. They punched her repeatedly and she tried to escape. But finally she just lay in a heap on the floor, curled in a fetal position. "All right boys, let's go." He gave Tasha a kick. "You ain't worth a dime looking like that. Call me when you get your shit together or we'll make permanent damage."

The three men left and Tasha stayed on the floor sobbing for several minutes. She finally got up and limped into the bathroom. She looked in the mirror and took stock of her face. It was red at this point, but she knew it would be black and blue and swollen if she didn't she get some ice on it. She could barely walk, but she managed to get to the kitchen and took the ice packs back to the sofa in the living room. She lay there with the ice packs for about half an hour. She pondered calling back the john she was supposed to have met that night, but Preacher Boy was right about one thing. She wasn't going to be in any shape to turn tricks anytime soon.

She got up slowly and limped back to the bathroom. She found some pain pills and sleeping pills and took them both. She hated the idea of sleeping in the bed where she had just been violated, but she had to lie down. She pulled off the covers and lay down on the sheets and closed her eyes. She prayed that the pills would work and she could sleep. Luckily, they did and she slept through the night.

6

LEO HAD A HARD TIME PAYING ATTENTION DURING THE DAY'S WORKSHOPS, BUT HE NEEDN'T WORRY ABOUT IT. He'd been a union organizer for twenty years and he knew the routine like the back of his hand. In fact, he was starting to feel that it might be time to move up in the organization or do something completely different. The only thing that kept him satisfied with his current position was the freshness of working with the cannabis industry. They were younger than the majority of union members, and most of them were clueless to the harsh working conditions of the distant past. Leo relished the idea of making them appreciative of what unions have done for the workforce. He hoped to get them energized enough to resurrect the glory days.

As he counted the hours until nine p.m., he thought about Tasha's desire to move. She made good money, but he could certainly understand why she'd want to leave Las Vegas. And he would be happy to bring her along with him to California.

After the dinner speaker had finished, he rushed off to his room to shower and dress. He got to the Bellagio just before nine and walked around the roulette tables, looking for Tasha. She wasn't dealing at any of the tables. He knew it wasn't kosher to ask about any particular dealer to security, but he noticed one of the other dealers leaving a table for a break. "Hey, excuse me, do you know where Tasha is?"

"She's out sick."

"Oh. Do you know how I can get in touch with her?"

"You don't have the number?"

"No."

The woman gave him a hard look. "Do you, uh, know her?"

"Yes. I just saw her last night." Leo could tell she wasn't buying it. "I thought I put the number in my phone last night but the contact isn't there."

A slight smirk crossed her face. "Try paying more attention to the business end of the arrangement next time."

"Uh . . ."

By the confused look on his face, she realized he wasn't quite what he seemed. "Okay, I can help a gentleman out from time to time.

Have you something to write on?" Leo fumbled through his pockets and found one of the business cards he had collected that day. "She won't be able to see you tonight, though," the woman said as she scribbled a number on the card and handed it back to him. She quickly walked away.

Leo took out his phone and immediately dialed. It went to Voicemail. "Tasha's phone. Leave your number."

"It's Leo. I'd like to come over. Maybe bring some chicken soup? Please call me right back."

He hung up and immediately his phone rang. "Hello Leo. I really can't see you right now."

"What's wrong? You seemed fine last night."

Tasha was silent for a minute. She sighed and finally said, "It came on suddenly after I saw you. I look terrible."

"I don't care. Just let me come over, please."

Silence hung between them. "Okay, I guess," She gave him the address.

"Do you want me to bring anything? Medicine? Food? Whiskey?"

"I'll be there as quick as I can." Leo rushed through the lobby, eager to get to her apartment. His phone showed that Tasha lived pretty close to the Strip, so once he made it out of the parking garage and down a nearby side street, it only took him a few more minutes to reach her complex. He knocked and waited for what seemed like several minutes before she opened the door just wide enough to let Leo slip through. Tasha held herself against the wall behind the door as if to hide, and it only took a glance back to see why. Her face was swollen black and blue. Sweatshirt and pants covered the rest of the damage. She was holding her arm in a makeshift sling and she stood with her other hand on her hip as if she was holding herself up. Leo gasped and went towards her, but she steeled herself, her body language making it plain that any touch would be painful. She limped by him and eased herself onto the sofa, wincing as she tried to make herself comfortable. "Tasha! What happened?" Leo asked. She started to cry and Leo went to sit next to her. She turned into him and sobbed. "Did you go the hospital? Maybe I need to take you —"

"No!" she interrupted. "I can't."

"Who did this to you?"

"Oh, Leo." She pulled away and turned toward him. "I don't just deal at the casino. I also . . . do other stuff . . . it puts a lot of cash into my savings account."

Leo felt slightly repulsed, but mostly angry. He wasn't sure at who . . . Tasha? Or all the men in the world who put women in these circumstances? Or was he jealous of all the men who had slept with her? "And one of them did this to you?"

"Oh no! I'm careful. I only go with men my gut tells me I can trust. I've never had a problem with a john."

"Then who beat you up like this?"

"There's this pimp trying to get me to work for him. I guess I said no once too often."

Leo shot up off the sofa. "And he beat you up because you wouldn't work for him?" he yelled angrily.

"Shhh," Tasha admonished him. "These walls are paper-thin."

Leo sat back down. "Sorry."

"It's okay. They've heard a lot already and never called the police."

"*You* need to call the police. He can't get away with this."

"C'mon Leo. So I can get arrested for prostitution?"

"I thought it was legal in Nevada."

"Not here in Las Vegas. Only in Pahrump, and a few other godforsaken counties. It's only legal at the end of the road."

"Then what are you going to do?"

"I won't work for him. But he does have goons who enjoyed watching him rape me and followed his orders to beat me."

"He raped you too?" Leo got up and paced. "He's not done, is he?"

Tasha shook her head. "No. He will never be done. He will be paying me visits until I agree."

"Then you need to leave right away."

"I think so," she replied, brushing tears off her cheek.

"I'll get you out of here. Are you afraid they'll come back tonight? I could bring you to my hotel room."

"I'm no use to them looking like this."

"I guess not."

"He told me to call him in a few days."

"Why?"

Tasha glared at Leo. "What do you think? To agree to work for him. Or else."

"Or else?" Both of them knew that Leo's question didn't need an answer.

"Thank you for coming over, Leo, but I took some pain pills and they're kicking in. I need to go to bed."

"Are you sure you want me to leave you alone?"

"I'm okay."

"What's this guy's name?"

She sighed. "Don't go there, Leo."

"Just tell me."

She lay down on the sofa and closed her eyes. "Preacher Boy Ray." Leo stood over Tasha and watched as her breathing steadied into a sound sleep. His asthma had kicked in with all of this so he took out his inhaler to steady his own breathing. He let himself out and stopped at a liquor store on his way back to the hotel. He bought a six-pack and a bag of peanuts. It might be a long night. He had a lot of planning to do.

Leo spent the next couple of hours on the phone. His first call was to Gordon, his best friend. They had grown up together in New York City, but were from different worlds. Leo was the product of an Italian father and Jewish mother, both of whom were progressive political activists. Their agenda leaned so far left that they had been labeled Communists by some members of New York's Democratic machine. Gordon had come from a poor African-American family, headed by a strong mother, with an absent father and a bunch of siblings from different men. The bond between the two boys had been based on their dislike of sports. They were curious about politics and racial injustice even at an early age. Gordon had spent many hours at Leo's family's dinner table, absorbing and relishing in the argumentative discourse that went on. The conversations about history and politics were always enlightening and a far cry from what went on in Gordon's house. His mother worked sixteen hours a day, leaving one of his older sisters in charge of putting some kind of dinner together and it was a rare occurrence that the siblings ate together. The house was always noisy and not conducive to studying, so Gordon spent as much time as he could at Leo's or the library.

They stayed in touch through college, but Leo was angry at Gordon's decision to go to law school. He thought Gordon was selling out, and there was a rift between them for a few years until Gordon decided to intern at the Equal Justice Initiative.

It was late, but Leo knew Gordon would always take his call. They had that kind of friendship. "Hey bro, I've got a problem," Leo said after the cursory hellos, how are yous, and what have you been up tos.

Gordon laughed. "And when don't you have a problem? Isn't that the life of a union organizer?"

"And your life as an attorney isn't?"

"Okay. So what do you need?"

"I'm in Las Vegas with the yearly convention. Remember that dealer I told you about? The one I talk to every year when I'm here?"

"Yeah. Tricia or something?"

"Tasha. Apparently she also turns tricks on the side. A pimp who's trying to get her to work for him beat her and raped her last night. Is there anything she can do legally without jeopardizing herself? She should still be able to press charges for assault, shouldn't she?"

"It's a touchy one. Prostitution isn't legal in Vegas and I doubt she'd get very far in the judicial system there. In fact, he may even be paying off the cops."

"So her only solution is to get out of town?"

"Probably."

"I thought so, but just wanted your opinion. I'm on my way to the Eureka area, so I'll take her with me."

"Why are you getting involved?" Gordon asked.

"I feel bad for her. She told me the night before this happened that she has a BA in Botany. I figured maybe she can find work in the pot industry up there."

Gordon laughed loudly. "Now that's funny. I wonder if anyone else up there has a degree in botany."

"The Emerald Triangle has changed now that it's legal. People are creating all kinds of strains for all kinds of uses. A botanist could be a real boon for some farm."

"You know, I actually know a place up there. You know that guy Luther I got the conviction overturned for?"

"Yeah, that was great work."

"He left a message that he's going to work on a pot farm in Garberville. Maybe she could start by talking to them."

"Fantastic! Do you have a phone number for him?"

Gordon gave Leo the phone number. "Give Luther a message for me, will you?"

"Sure."

"Just tell him to make sure he stays in the legal end of the industry. He doesn't need any marks on his record."

"I'll tell him Judge Gordon is watching him."

Gordon snorted. "Keep in touch. How long are you going to be up there?"

"I'm never sure."

"I don't know how you do it, always living out of a suitcase."

"I like it. No ties."

"I don't know about that. It sounds like you're getting tied up with this Tasha. Watch your step. These Vegas pimps are bad news."

"I've got ways of dealing with them too."

"I know you do. That's what I'm talking about. Just watch your step and don't do anything stupid. I know you too well. You tend to go overboard when you're smitten."

"Who says I'm smitten?" Leo said defensively.

"You're not that nice a guy. You wouldn't be doing this for Tasha if you weren't." And with that, Gordon hung up.

Leo wanted to call Luther next, but it was late. He'd wait until the morning. His next calls were to some cronies in East St. Louis. He explained what was going on and asked them when they could get to Vegas. He had a plan and he knew he needed to use people who weren't on the West Coast.

They said they could be there in a couple of days. Good. That would give Leo time to talk to Luther and get Tasha situated. Things were falling into place nicely. Leo looked at the clock and found he could still get a few hours of sleep before the keynote speaker at nine.

7

LEO CALLED LUTHER DURING THE MORNING COFFEE BREAK, BUT IT WENT TO VOICEMAIL. He left a message explaining that he was a friend of Gordon's and was on his way to Garberville. Next call was to Tasha and that also went to voicemail. He worried that something had happened to her, so he decided to go to her apartment right away. He rushed out and was knocking on her door within half an hour. There was no answer and he started yelling through the door. Finally she opened the door. "Jeez, Leo. Do you have to make such a racket?" she yawned, hanging on the doorknob.

"I was afraid he had come back. You didn't answer the phone."

"I was still sleeping. Those pills are strong." She smiled. "But thanks for caring." Tasha leaned back and let Leo pass by her.

"I think I have a place for you to go." He told her about his call to Gordon. "I still haven't reached Luther, but hopefully he'll call back soon and we can find out more."

"Thanks, Leo. Now, don't you have to get back to the conference? I'd like to get back to sleep and see you when I'm feeling better."

"I'll come back tonight around six. We can go out to dinner."

"Uh, Leo," she said, motioning to her disfigured face.

"Then I'll bring us dinner."

Tasha managed a painful little smile. "That'd be great."

Leo spent the rest of the day at the conference working on his plan for dealing with Preacher Boy Ray, forgetting completely about organizing the cannabis workers. He wanted to know exactly what he was going to do when he talked to Tasha that evening, even though he would not be sharing all of it with her. She didn't need to know exactly what these "friends" from East St. Louis were going to do.

He slipped out of the conference a little early to change and pick up dinner. He wanted to bring a nice dinner, not his usual fare of pizza, Chinese food, or hamburgers. He had never frequented nice restaurants in Las Vegas other than those at the hotels holding the conference, and he also had no idea what Tasha liked. He almost called her but finally realized he was making way too much of it. He just stopped at a supermarket and got a cooked chicken, a couple of packaged salads, a loaf of French bread and a bottle of wine.

Tasha was a little concerned about drinking wine with the pain pills she was taking, but Leo talked her into it. After finishing their first glass, they started on dinner and the conversation turned from small talk about how she was feeling and whether or not she should see a doctor to the issue at hand. "I have a plan," Leo said.

"Okay. What is it?"

"When you call Preacher Boy Ray, tell him you will work for him."

"Why? I'm not going to."

"I know. But I want you to plan a meeting with him somewhere. Not here. I'll figure out the place."

Tasha sighed. "I don't like the sound of this."

"Just make him think you will and plan to meet him to work out the details. I'll take care of the rest."

"What's the rest?"

"It doesn't matter," Leo replied quickly.

"It does matter, Leo. He's a very dangerous man. You can't just talk to him."

"I'm not going to talk to him."

"Then what are you going to do?"

Leo hesitated before answering. "I'm going to give him money," he lied.

She looked at him incredulously. "Why would you do that?"

"To keep him off your back," Leo replied, overriding his inner thoughts.

"But if I'm going to leave town anyway, why can't we just go?"

"Money talks."

"Ha! Leo, he'd have no problem taking your money and having us both killed. These aren't the nice guys you're used to dealing with."

Leo chuckled. "What makes you think I only work with nice guys?" Tasha gave him a sour look, but he didn't want to elaborate any more about the occasional connections between unions and the mob. Tasha was too young to know about Jimmy Hoffa. Leo kept his nose clean, but he had friends who did not. "Don't worry. Just do what I say."

"I've heard that one before."

Leo turned away. "You've just got to trust me, Tasha."

"I'm a little more desperate than trusting at this point."

He turned back. "Make the call and arrange to meet with him."

Tasha looked over the remains of their dinner. It all seemed so cute and naïve. "When?"

"I'll let you know. Just make whatever arrangements you need about your job and your apartment and then pack your bags."

Tasha sighed. "Leo, I'm running for my life. Who gives a shit about my job and my deposit?"

Leo winced. "I mean just be ready to go."

"I hope you know what you're doing."

"I know exactly what I'm doing." He smiled and reached out to touch her black and blue arm. Tasha grabbed his hand and rubbed her thumb over his palm.

"Thanks for dinner, but I'm going to take a pain pill and go to bed."

Leo stared at his hand as her thumb came to a stop. "I'll make the arrangements and let you know when to call him."

Tasha nodded slightly and let go of his hand. "Good night, Leo."

Leo returned to his hotel room and cancelled his plane ticket. Next he worked on where Tasha should plan the meeting with the pimp. He studied Google maps, considering the best place for everything to take place outside the glare of Vegas. Then it came to him. He had it all figured out. He lay his head down on the pillow and closed his eyes. Things were falling into place. A couple of days ago he flew into town expecting to see some old union friends and to check in with Tasha. She had been someone he saw once a year and enjoyed chatting with. Now he was falling for her, even traveling with her . . . and getting himself involved with a Las Vegas pimp and some shady people. Despite the butterflies in his stomach, he dozed off.

A text awoke Leo with a start. It was the East St Louis duo. They'd be there that night and were waiting for instructions. Leo texted back that he'd have everything figured out in a couple of hours. He checked the time. He would be late for the first workshop if he didn't get going and he didn't want to miss anything today. Tomorrow was the last day of the conference and he would not be attending. If all went as planned, he'd be on the road tonight.

He dialed Tasha and relayed the plan. "Call me after you've talked to Preacher Boy Ray and let me know the meeting time."

She called back within minutes. "All set for nine at Barney's Lounge."

"He didn't balk at meeting at the airport?"

"No. He bought the story that I was seeing a friend off." Or at least pretended to, she thought.

"Good. Okay I'll see you at nine." Leo texted his pals and asked them to be at Barney's a little earlier than that.

The afternoon went slowly, but it was finally six and Leo rushed back to his hotel room to pack. He picked up Tasha and the two of them got to McCarran International Airport about eight. First stop was Hertz. He asked if he could leave the car there for an hour or so. They took the shuttle to the terminal. "You go inside Barney's first," Leo said. "I'll come in and sit at the bar."

Tasha nodded and went inside, scanning the crowd until she noticed Preacher Boy Ray sitting at a table with his two goons. She walked over and slid into the booth without acknowledging any of them.

"What can I get you to drink, Tasha?" Preacher Boy said with a sardonic smirk.

"Poison," she answered. "And I don't mean a cocktail named Poison."

"Ooo-kay," Preacher Boy said, rolling his eyes. "So what do you have to say for yourself?"

She took a deep breath. "What's the split if I work for you?"

Preacher Boy snickered. "You finally came to your senses."

"I asked you a question," Tasha replied.

"Fifty-fifty if you use your apartment."

"So I keep doing what I've been doing but now I give you half of what I get. Hmmm." She pretended to look pensive. "Doesn't sound quite right."

"Hey, I give you protection and johns."

"I've got plenty of johns. I don't need your help."

"I can get you enough so you can quit your other job."

"I like dealing."

"I'll take care of you, Tasha. No one can hurt you."

"No one ever has except you!" she retorted. Preacher Boy Ray leaned back into the back of the seat with a smug grin. His goons followed suit. "Anyway, what do you want with me? I'm way past thirteen."

"There are always some customers who like screwing a veteran."

Tasha shook her head in disgust. "Well, that may be, but they're not going to want me looking like a prisoner of war."

"I'll give you another couple of days to get that swelling down. You can use make up for the bruising."

Tasha stood and glared at Preacher Boy. She wanted to have the last word but realized she had to stop somewhere. She hated that Leo was giving him money and deep down, she wasn't sure it would work. She turned abruptly and walked away, winking at Leo as she strolled by the bar, innocent of the fact that the two guys sitting next to him were also part of the plan.

Preacher Boy Ray swigged down the rest of his drink and threw some money on the table.

He stood to leave, watching Tasha walk towards the baggage claim. "We already gave that bitch her fifty percent, didn't we boys? We'll have to pay her another little social call and give her the other half." His goons laughed and followed him out of Barney's to the elevator that would take them to the parking garage. Leo and his buddies followed them out, but Leo turned and walked toward baggage claim where Tasha would be waiting for him. His pals from East St Louis would take care of the rest. Leo had cautioned them to go easy; just scare them enough to make them know that the next step would be a lot worse if they didn't leave Tasha alone.

Leo and Tasha eyed one another, but went separately to the shuttle that would take them to Hertz. Leo took out his inhaler and was finally able to breathe deeply.

8

THEY GOT IN THE CAR AND DIDN'T SPEAK UNTIL LEO HAD MERGED ONTO ROUTE 15 SOUTH. They would drive all night to Sacramento where they could recharge at Leo's. "My apartment isn't much since I'm never there. It's just a studio in midtown."

"You mean you're not living in a trendy neighborhood?" She winked at him.

"Well, it kind of is now, but I was there long before it became the hip place to live and rents got crazy."

"Does it have a bed, a shower, a coffee maker, and a microwave?"

"All of the above."

"That's all we need to recharge and get back on the road."

"True."

"How much did you give him?" she asked.

"Don't worry about it."

"I want to pay you back."

"You don't need to."

"Leo, I can't let you do that."

"Just forget it."

She shrugged. "How far is the drive to Sacramento?"

"Nine hours. How are you feeling?"

"Mentally or physically?" she answered.

"Both."

"Mentally great. Physically I've been better."

"Go ahead and take another pain pill if you want. You can sleep. I'm fine to drive."

"No. I want to be able to help you drive if you need a break. I might close my eyes, but I don't want to take another pill." She adjusted the seat back and scrunched up her jacket to use as a pillow and was asleep in less than a minute.

Leo debated about whether to turn the radio on. He didn't want to wake her up, but he needed something to help him keep his eyes open while driving through the desert in the dark. No station came in all that clearly, and that probably was just as well. Those that did were either touting evangelical Christianity or conspiracy theory.

He drove for about an hour before his eyelids started to droop. He looked over at Tasha, but she seemed to be in a deep sleep. He thought about what lay ahead, trying to think pleasant thoughts. It was better than thinking about what had just occurred. Unfortunately, he was pulled back in when his phone dinged. He took it out and glanced at it. "Done. They won't be bothering you. Call me tomorrow." Leo felt a little uneasy, worrying that they might have gone too far. He'd find out in the morning.

After another hour he realized he'd need to pull over and get recharged. He stopped at the next open gas station and started pumping gas. He opened the passenger door and woke Tasha. "Do you need to use the rest room? This gas station looks decent."

"Yeah, that would be good." She got out and walked a bit unsteadily toward the door.

Leo ran up to her and held her arm. "You okay?"

"These pills must last longer than I thought."

"They probably stay in your system for more than a day."

"Where are we?"

"Just outside of Barstow," Leo answered as he let go of her arm in front of the restroom door and tried the door. "I guess you need a key. Wait here." He went inside the station and came out with the key. "I'll use it after you."

She came out after a few minutes and held the door for Leo. "I'll meet you inside."

Leo joined her inside and bought them some coffee. "Do you want something to eat?" he asked.

"Coffee's fine. I can drive for awhile."

"Are you sure?" He wanted her to drive because he was tired and would love to get some shuteye, but he was concerned that the pills were still affecting her.

"Yeah, I'm fine. What's to worry about? We're in the desert. No cars, nothing to hit." She laughed as she looked at Leo's furrowed brow. "I'm kidding."

He smiled, though a bit uneasily. "Okay. Maybe I'll take a short nap."

She took the keys. They got in the car and she took off. Leo was asleep in a flash. He opened his eyes and looked out the window. He was surprised to see some very familiar sights. "We're already in Stockton?" he exclaimed.

"You slept well. And guess what? I didn't hit anything along the way!" she laughed.

"What time is it?"

"About six I think."

"We'll be in Sacramento in less than an hour. Pull over and let me drive the rest of the way."

"Yeah, we need gas anyway and besides, I don't know where your apartment is." She pulled into a gas station and they used the restroom and changed drivers.

They arrived at his apartment before seven. "Sorry about the mess. I wasn't expecting company when I left a week ago."

Tasha laughed. "I'm sure this week turned out quite differently than you had anticipated."

"Do you want to sleep or shower or eat?"

"That's a hard choice. They are all enticing. Maybe sleep." She looked at the sofa bed. "This pulls out into a bed, I presume?" Leo jumped into action. He opened the sofa and took the blanket and pillows out of the closet. Tasha had gone into the bathroom and when she came out, she was in her underwear. She got into bed and smiled at Leo. "Are you going to join me?"

"I could. I mean . . ." He stumbled over his words, sounding more and more foolish. He went to the bathroom and he, too, came out in his underwear. He climbed in next to her, but she had already fallen asleep. He turned onto his side and sighed as he closed his eyes.

When Tasha woke up Leo was dressed and sitting at the table with a bag from Freeport Bakery in front of him and the coffeemaker dripping. "Did you get us some goodies? I'm starving." She took a couple of bites out of a pastry and said, "Actually, I think I'll shower before breakfast."

"There are towels on the shelf in there," Leo called out to her as he watched her go in and shut the door. He took the opportunity to call the East Saint Louis pair. "How did things go?"

"Perfectly. Got them outside their car in the garage. No one was around."

"What do you mean 'got them'?" Leo asked, apprehensively.

"Let's just say they won't be running any marathons for a while."

"They're alive, right?"

"Yeah, Leo. Who do you think we are?"

"Just making sure. Thanks. I owe you."

"No problem."

Leo hung up just as Tasha came out of the bathroom. They ate their breakfast and talked about nothing in particular. "We can take the rental back on the way north. My car's in a garage a couple of blocks from here," Leo said.

"I'd better drive your car since I wasn't on the rental contract," she replied. It didn't take long to get ready and they were on the road again by noon.

It was dark when Leo and Tasha arrived in Garberville. They went immediately to a restaurant to get a bite to eat and try Luther again. He hadn't called back, and Leo had no idea whether or not they would be welcome to stay at this farm. It went to voicemail . . . again. "I'm going to call Gordon and see what he thinks is going on." He dialed. "Gordon? Luther hasn't answered any of my calls. We're in Garberville now. Are you sure he's talked to the guy who owns the farm?"

"I don't know. Haven't talked to him. Do you want me to call him?"

"Would you mind?"

"I'll try."

Leo hung up and turned to Tasha. "I think we should get a motel room for tonight."

"Probably a good idea. There's one right across the street. It's not exactly classy, but it'll do for one night."

"I doubt there's going to be anything in either Garberville or Eureka that will hold a candle to the Bellagio."

"I like it here," she said looking around the restaurant. "Real people. Maybe not beautiful, but earthy."

"Are Las Vegas people beautiful?"

"They work at it. Maybe not beautiful in your eyes, if fake boobs and fake eyelashes don't turn you on."

"You're not like that and you're beautiful." Leo was surprised that came out of his mouth. He hoped Tasha wouldn't take it wrong. He didn't want to come on too strong. Luckily Tasha seemed to ignore the statement.

"I'd just as soon have a low-key restful night anyway. A lot has happened and I'm not that up to meeting new people who may or may not be glad to see us."

"Good point. Let's just plan on staying in the motel tonight and look for this farm in the morning." Leo paid the bill and they walked across the street to check in.

It wasn't until after they had been in the room for a couple of hours that Gordon called. "Leo, I haven't reached Luther either. Maybe cell service isn't that great there, but I tend to think he isn't used to checking his phone. Especially since he isn't expecting any calls. I'll keep trying."

"Thanks Gordon. I appreciate it." Leo hung up and relayed the news to Tasha. "I have lists of pot farms, the ones I had planned to go to for organizing, and so we actually have a lot of choices here. It doesn't have to be that one. It's not harvest season, though. We can go on to Eureka. I have a couple of meetings there already set up so I'll need to go anyway. It's by the ocean, but cold. It's not like southern California."

"Sounds fine to me." Tasha sighed. "I'm just glad to be out of Vegas."

Leo nodded. They had rented a room with two double beds. Tasha was in one of them and Leo had been sitting in a chair. He wanted to get into bed with her, but thought he should wait for an invitation. She had invited him in last night, but this was a different situation. There was a choice. "I guess I'll take my shower now," he said.

"Okay. I'll go after you."

Leo grinned as he shut the door to the bathroom. Perfect. Then the choice would be hers to make. Unfortunately, it didn't happen that way. Tasha was fast asleep when he opened the bathroom door.

THE FARM

9

JUNIPER LEFT THE CANADIANS AT THE BUS STOP AND PULLED UP IN FRONT OF THE EEL CAFÉ. She started to get out of the truck and paused, realizing that Dutch had not given her a description of Luther. She frowned, but perhaps he'd be easy to spot because harvest was over and most of the seasonal workers had left town. She was right. When she opened the café door and glanced around, there was only one youngish person in a room full of old Garberville denizens and maybe a couple of stray tourists from the Benbow Inn. But more than that, he was the only black man in a part of California that didn't see many. She walked to his table and quietly asked, "Luther?"

He looked up and saw a beautiful woman about his age with a warm smile, but eyes that seemed older, wiser, and warier. "Yes?"

"I'm Juniper. I'm here to give you a ride to Dutch's farm."

"Oh." He smiled as he let out the breath he didn't realize he was holding, another reminder of how much he had to let go of after twenty years of constantly being vigilant. "Thanks." He stood and hoisted his backpack and deposited his coffee cup in the trash.

"I have to stop at the grocery store and natural foods store before we leave."

"Okay. That's cool." He followed her to the truck and opened the door to the passenger side.

"We can walk. It's only a couple of blocks. I'm just getting my bags."

"You bring your own bags to the grocery store?"

Juniper looked at him quizzically. "Where have you been? You're not from California?" Luther didn't know how to respond so he said nothing. "It's the law now. You need to bring your own bags or pay for them . . . for the environment." He shrugged but still stayed silent. "You can leave your backpack in the cab, if you want. I'll lock it."

"That's okay. I'll hang on to it."

"Suit yourself, but you have nothing to worry about. We won't be gone that long." She walked up Maple Lane towards the natural food store with Luther following along like a puppy dog. He felt awkward and nervous in the presence of this woman who seemed so self-assured. He had not been around women for many years and he hadn't had much experience with girls in high school anyway.

He wandered around the natural foods store in a bit of a daze, studying foods he never heard of before. No doubt there were such stores in Oakland, but certainly not in his neighborhood. Juniper finished her shopping and beckoned him. They walked to Ray's Food Place, the town supermarket, without a word. He wanted to talk but didn't have a clue what to say. He assumed Jed had told Dutch his whole story, but apparently Dutch hadn't told it to Juniper. "Did Dutch tell you where I've been for the last twenty years?" he finally blurted out.

Juniper stopped walking and stared at him. "No. Should he have?"

"I – I – I don't know." He laughed. "I guess I have to tell you now."

She nodded her head slowly. "Yeah, I guess you do."

"I've been in prison for the last twenty years." He waited for a negative reaction, but she only tilted her head slightly and smiled.

"Well, I guess that explains why you didn't know about the ban on single use bags."

"I was exonerated. I didn't commit the crime."

"Congratulations." She reconsidered her remark. "Is that the appropriate reaction?"

"Congratulations is fine." They arrived at Ray's and she grabbed a shopping cart. "I don't have any money for groceries. I'm hoping to earn it working for Dutch," Luther explained as they walked through the automatic doors.

"Dutch has more than he needs. There are others staying at the farm besides you. Taking in others seems to have become a hobby of his."

"Jed told me about Homer."

"There are also a couple of others: Scarlett and Buster."

"How long have they lived there?"

"They just arrived. You might have heard of Buster Fingerpickin' McCracken?"

"My mother used to listen to his music. Wow. He's at the farm? Man, how old is he?"

"I don't know." She smiled. "Old."

"And who's Scarlett?" Juniper thought for a while about how much to reveal to Luther. "Sorry," Luther finally said. "Maybe I shouldn't have asked."

"No. You're fine. It's just difficult and not really my story to share. But it's better if you know. Scarlett was my younger foster sister and ended up entangled in a sex ring after I was released from the system. I only found out recently, and I managed to get her out and bring her here." Luther let out a nervous laugh and quickly covered his mouth. "I take it you weren't imprisoned over a trumped-up sex charge," she retorted.

"Yeah — I mean, sorry. I'm just sort of relieved I won't be the only one there with a past."

"Understandable," mused Juniper as she studied the expiration dates on jugs of milk.

They finished the shopping and struggled back to the car, overloaded with grocery bags. "I guess I should have left my backpack in the car. How far is the farm?"

"Twenty or thirty minutes."

"Not exactly walking distance, I guess."

"Not really."

They drove in silence for a few minutes until Luther finally broke it. "Well, how about you? What's your story?"

"You mean how did I end up on the farm? What's in my sordid past?"

"I wasn't saying that exactly. Just trying to get to know you."

She sighed. "I was a trimmer first. I liked living here so I moved in full time and I'm in charge of the trimmers and the household stuff."

"So you and Dutch are —"

"No!" she interrupted. "We are not."

Luther smiled, as he was quite happy to hear that. "Are you from San Francisco?"

"Yes, but I left and spent several years traveling. Are you from the city too?"

"Oakland."

"Is your family still there?"

"My mother died when I was in prison. She was the only one who cared about me."

"I guess we have much in common," Juniper said softly.

"Seems like it."

They arrived at the locked gate leading to the driveway up to the farm. Juniper punched in the code and they drove up to the house. "This place is awesome!" Luther exclaimed. "I never saw anything like this before, even before San Quentin."

"It's pretty special, even if you didn't spend time in jail." She parked the car and they grabbed the groceries and went into the kitchen. Homer and Buster were in there attempting to make lunch. "Hey guys, this is Luther."

"How ya doin' Luther? I'm Buster, this here's Homer." Buster put his hand out.

Luther shook it. "My mother used to listen to you all the time. It's a real pleasure." He turned to Homer. "Homer, I have a message for you from Jed. He said he's going to come up soon to see you."

"You know Jed? Special man. Very special," Homer said.

"Yes, he is." Luther turned to Juniper. "Can I help you put the groceries away?"

"No, that's fine. Why don't you join Buster and Homer for lunch."

"Good luck finding anything to eat around here," Homer said. "They ain't got nothing but healthy crap."

"Homer, you have enough preservatives in you to last two lifetimes," Juniper teased.

"I'm making us some grilled cheese sandwiches. You want some, Luther?" Buster asked.

"Yeah, that would be great."

"Sit down and keep Homer company. I'll have to find Dutch and see what room he wants to put you in," Juniper said.

"I have my own room?" Luther asked. "How many bedrooms you got here?"

"More than you've ever seen in any one house, I bet," Homer said. "We all got our own rooms. Bet you think you died and went to heaven."

"Something like that," Luther grinned.

Dutch came in at that moment and smiled at Luther. "How ya doin' Luther. I'm Dutch."

Luther scrambled to a standing position, almost knocking over his chair. "Oh, man, thanks so much for letting me come."

Dutch just nodded. "Finish eating and then come into my music room." He turned to Homer. "Do you need anything?"

"Nah, I have a full pipe in my room. I'm taking a nap after lunch."

Dutch nodded again and left the room. "He doesn't talk much?" Luther asked Homer.

"He keeps his distance. But he's a good man."

"I can see that," Luther said, sitting down as Buster put a plate down in front of him.

10

DUTCH WAS STRUMMING HIS GUITAR AND SMOKING A JOINT WHEN LUTHER ENTERED THE MUSIC ROOM. He offered the joint and Luther took a couple of hits. "Do you want me to give you a tour of the farm now or see your room?" Dutch asked.

"I'd like to see the farm." Just as they were about to leave, Luther's phone rang. He recognized the number as Gordon's. "I need to answer this. It's my lawyer." Dutch shot him a wary glance. "Nothing's wrong, I'm sure," Luther added hastily. "Hello?"

"Hey, Luther. It's Gordon. I've been trying to get a hold of you. Don't you check your messages?"

"Sorry. I, uh, just haven't gotten the hang of carrying a phone yet."

Gordon laughed. "That's what I figured. A good friend of mine is in Garberville and needs a place for a lady friend of his to stay. She needs to be under the radar for a bit. I was hoping you could ask that guy Dutch if she could stay there. Listen to your messages. His name is Leo and he's been trying to call you and text you too. He's going to buy you some minutes when he gets there, so would you please call him?"

Luther noticed Dutch was waiting impatiently. This would not be a good time to ask about adding to his collection of misfits. I'm sorry, Gordon. I'm just now going out with Dutch to take in the farm and see what I can do for him. I'll call when we're done."

"Thanks, Luther. I don't mean to put you in an awkward position."

"I know. It's okay. Payback time." Luther studied the keypad before finding the right button to end the call, and then turned to Dutch. "Let's go."

They walked for about half an hour, checking out the growing area, a pond, a vegetable garden, and a small orchard. The rest of the property was old pasture and trees as far as their eyes could see. It was lush and beautiful. "How much land do you have?" Luther asked.

"Eighty acres."

"Whoa. That's a lot of land. How much do you use for growing pot?"

"A couple of acres."

"You have all this land and you don't do anything with it?"

"What do you think I should do with it?" countered Dutch.

"Well, uh — maybe build some houses on some of it and sell 'em."

"I came here to get away from that."

"Yeah, I get it."

"Will you miss the nightlife living out here in the boondocks?" Dutch asked.

Luther thought about that Pub Crawl with the hostel guests and wondered if he might, in fact, wish for some of that. But he knew better than to express any drawbacks to the living situation. "Nah."

"Good. Let's go back. I have some work to do."

"Is there anything I can help you with? I'm ready to do whatever you need," Luther said.

"Talk to Juniper and see if she has anything. Maybe you can help with Homer, since she has her hands full with Scarlett."

They got back to the house and Dutch showed Luther his room. It was sparsely furnished with a bed, a dresser, and a lamp. Luther couldn't believe how big the room was compared not only to his cell, but also to his room at the hostel. There were a couple of wall hangings and some sort of waterfall fountain made from rocks sitting on the dresser. "This is great," he said as he studied the fountain.

"It's for relaxation," Dutch said. "You can put it in the closet if you don't want it."

"No, I like it." Dutch left and Luther decided he should call this Leo guy back. He felt quite proud of himself once he figured out how to call back the person who left a voicemail. "Hello? This is Luther."

"Oh, man, thanks for calling," Leo answered. "Gordon told me you're feeling a little weird about asking Dutch. Did Gordon tell you that I'm a union organizer? I was going to use that as a form of introduction so you don't have to be involved much."

"I don't know," Luther replied. "Maybe that would be a good idea, but things are pretty quiet around here. I don't think anyone is unhappy with the working conditions. I'll call you as soon as I've talked to him."

"Okay, Luther. Much appreciated. I look forward to meeting you. Oh, and be sure to tell him my lady friend has a degree in botany."

Luther hung up and closed his eyes. He was tired and wanted to take a nap, but he had to see what Dutch had to say about adding another person to the ever-expanding farm population. Just then there was a knock on his door. "Come in."

Juniper opened the door and stood there. "Were you sleeping?" she asked.

Luther sat up hastily. "Oh no. I wasn't asleep."

"Sorry it's taken me so long to get back with you," she said, still standing at the door.

"That's okay. You've been busy with, uh, is it Scarlett?"

Juniper sighed. "Yeah, Scarlett. She's pretty sick."

"What's wrong with her?"

"She's a junkie, for one thing, although it's not of her own doing."

"Huh? How does one become an addict if they're not doing it to themselves?"

"She was drugged in that cult."

"Shit. So you went to San Francisco to save her . . ."

"Sort of. I picked her up there, anyway. I'm not sure if I saved her yet." They were quiet for a minute or so.

"Juniper?"

"Yes?"

"I'd like to tell you my story."

Juniper shut the door and came to sit on the bed next to Luther. "Okay. Shoot."

"The summer after I graduated from high school I was in a car with some guys I barely knew. They ended up robbing a convenience store and murdering the owner. I wasn't even inside the store when it happened, but I was the one there when the cops came. I was arrested and put in jail and then convicted for the crime."

"What happened to the other guys?"

"One was killed inside the store. The other guy shot the owner and then ran away. I went inside to see what had happened and that's where they found me."

"Where was the gun? Weren't the other guy's fingerprints on it?"

"He was wearing gloves. He just threw the gun on the floor and ran. I had just been playing basketball with them and didn't even know their names."

"So what happened? Were you finally acquitted?"

"I was finally exonerated. It took The Innocence Project years to push my case through."

"So how long have you been out?"

"Less than a week."

Juniper smiled. "I'm glad this worked out for you. I have a pretty good idea of what it is like to be let loose with few resources."

"I'm very grateful." Luther exhaled. "You know, maybe you can help me. It's sorta like Scarlett's situation."

"What's that?"

"This guy who's a friend of my lawyer is coming with some lady from Vegas who's on the run from some pimp or something. The guy's a union organizer. I don't know much of the story, but Gordon, that's my lawyer, asked if they could come for a visit. Oh, and she has a degree in — uh, botany." Luther fidgeted. "I guess she needs a place to stay and hide for a little while."

"And you haven't asked Dutch yet?"

"No."

"When are they coming?"

"They're already in Garberville."

Juniper frowned and stood. "I'd better go talk to Dutch."

"Can I help with Homer while you do that? I asked Dutch if there was any work I could do right now. He said I should take care of Homer since you're dealing with Scarlett."

"Homer's not exactly an invalid, you know."

Luther looked away. "I'm just telling you what Dutch said."

Juniper started to walk out of the room. "Well, come on with me and you can ask Homer yourself." Luther followed her out, as perplexed as ever about what to do and how Juniper felt about him or anything else, for that matter. She pointed to a door. "He's in there. See if he wants anything." Luther watched her walk away.

He knocked. "Homer? This is Luther. We met earlier?" There was no response so Luther knocked more loudly.

"Come in!" Homer shouted.

Luther opened the door and saw Homer dancing around the room with headphones on, holding something that looked like a tiny Walkman. Luther smiled. "What are you listening to?" he practically yelled.

"Juniper put some of Dutch's music on this for me. Now I need to get some young'un like you to put Buster's music on for me." Homer shoved the iPod into Luther's hands.

Luther looked down and shook his head and chuckled. "Hell, this is too small to stick a cassette in somewhere, let alone a CD."

"Hah! I thought all you kids knew how to do this stuff."

"Not all of us, I guess. We'll learn together."

Homer took the headphones off and sat down. He patted the bed next to him for Luther to sit down. "So, young fella, what's your story?"

Luther sat down and took a deep breath. He knew this was going to happen a lot. He had to be honest with people. His thoughts of getting away from it all and hiding was not going to work. Certainly the people he was going to be living with had a right to know. "I've been in prison for the last twenty years for a murder I did not commit. I've been vindicated. I'm trying —"

Homer stopped him. "That's all you gotta say. You didn't kill anybody and now you're free. No need to explain anymore. I got it."

Luther smiled appreciatively. "Thanks. It gets tiresome."

"I'm sure it does. I have Parkinson's disease and that's all you need to know. Right?"

"Right."

Homer put his hand up for a high five and Luther slapped it. "Now, let's go see if we can find someone to help us put Buster's music on my iPod." Homer stood and teetered. Luther grabbed his elbow and steadied him. "You'll get used to me, Luther."

Luther nodded. "Just let me know what you need."

"Actually, I could use some more weed. Could you ask Juniper for some of that Kobain Kush?"

"Okay. I'll be right back." Luther left to find Juniper. He had no luck so he knocked on Dutch's music room door.

"Yeah?" Dutch said.

"It's Luther. I can't find Juniper and Homer needs some Kobain Kush."

"Come on in." Luther entered timidly. "I'll get some ready for you. If Kurt only knew what he created for Parkinson's patients," Dutch chuckled.

"Kurt?" Luther asked.

Dutch looked at him in disbelief. "You never heard of Kurt Cobain? Nirvana?"

"I've heard of them. I just didn't put it together. Did you know him? Is that why you named it after him?"

"Kush is a Hindu name for marijuana. Kobain Kush is an Indica dominant strain high in THC. It's a hybrid. I don't know who came up with the name, but it wasn't me. But yes, I knew him. He wasn't in my world, though. Different music . . . a different era." He handed Luther a vaporizer. "Homer knows what to do. Just stay with him while he takes it. I'm still trying to monitor the dosage."

"Okay, thanks. By the way, Homer wants to put some of Buster's music on his, uh, Walkman thingy."

Dutch laughed. "Okay. Bring it to me. I'll download some for him."

"Can I watch when you do?"

"Why?"

Luther shrugged and smiled sheepishly. "I have a lot to learn."

"I get it. But I'll teach you later. I've got to finish some work here."

"Has Juniper talked to you?"

"About?"

"Oh, I'll let her tell you."

Luther left and returned to Homer's room. "I've got a vaporizer all ready for you." He handed it to Homer and watched as Homer's trembling hand held the vaporizer to his mouth

and inhaled. He held it in for a few seconds
before exhaling. It didn't take long for Homer's
hands to stop shaking. He continued vaping and
then grinned at Luther. "Let's see if we can find
a snack."

11

"THERE'S NEVER ANYTHING GOOD TO EAT HERE," HOMER COMPLAINED AS HE RUMMAGED THROUGH THE REFRIGERATOR AND THE KITCHEN CABINETS.

"What do you mean?" Luther laughed. There's plenty of food."

"It's all too damn healthy!"

Luther's phone buzzed. "Hello?"

"Hey Luther, it's Leo. Have you talked to Dutch yet? We're at the gate."

"Oh man! No I haven't talked to him. I didn't think you were going to come until I had let you know that I had asked Dutch."

"I know, but I found the address of the farm in my union organizing list and we thought we'd take a ride up here. It's okay. We can stay at the motel."

Luther felt bad that he had been too chicken to talk to Dutch. "If you want to wait at the gate I can see if I can find him."

"Thanks. That would be great. No problem waiting — the scenery is beautiful here."

Luther hung up. "You okay Homer? I have to find Juniper or Dutch."

"Yeah. Is that someone at the gate? See if he has some good old fashioned junk food, will you?"

Luther laughed. "We'll have to plan some secret shopping in the future." Luther wandered around the house looking for Juniper, but to no avail. He hated asking Dutch for anything, but he had no choice. "Dutch?" he practically whispered as he knocked.

"What now, Luther?"

Luther opened the door slightly but didn't go in. "I'm really sorry, but I can't find Juniper. People are at the gate and I don't know the code."

"Are those the friends of yours that Juniper told me about? One of them knows botany, right?"

Luther breathed a sigh of relief. "Yes, but they're not exactly friends of mine. Friends of my lawyer."

Dutch stood up. "I'll let them in. I need a walk anyway."

"Can I go with you?"

Dutch scowled for a moment. "Okay, but don't think your presence will sway me one way or another."

Luther bit his lip and stepped back to let Dutch through. Dutch took a key from around his neck and locked the music room door. They walked down the gravel road that curved and dipped through the forest to the gate. Luther studied the shadows on the ground before him as he walked slightly behind Dutch. There were things he wanted to say, but he knew he better not express them just now. Like Juniper, Dutch was a hard read. Down at the gate stood a couple, leaning against a car. Dutch lifted the lid on the control box and punched in the code and the gate slowly swung open. The man came forward and extended his hand.

"I'm Leo," he said and looking over his shoulder as a way to lure her forward, "and this is my friend, Tasha."

Dutch ignored Leo's outstretched hand. "I'm Dutch. I own this place. Drive on up to the house and we'll meet you in a few minutes."

"There's room in the back seat —" Leo began.

"We'll meet you in a few minutes," Dutch repeated. Leo swallowed and nodded. They got back in the car and he started the engine and came through, driving carefully toward the house. "This way," Dutch said to Luther, jerking his head towards a side road. Luther followed, eager to be of service. Around a bend a large old barn appeared. Dutch went to the huge doors and pulled them open on their screaming hinges.

"So this is what the inside of a barn looks like," Luther said as he peered inside. It had twelve stalls, a hayloft, a tack room and layer upon layer of dust on everything.

"I have some ideas for what I want to do in this barn. First thing it needs, though, is a thorough cleaning."

"Are you going to get some horses?" Luther asked, suddenly recalling some dim boyhood thought.

Dutch didn't answer right away. Finally he responded. "As I said, I have some ideas. Are you up for the job?"

"Sure. I had a lot of experience with a mop and a broom the last twenty years."

Dutch nodded. "This isn't all about cleaning. You will need to get rid of the raccoons and rat nests and whatever else is in the old hay." Dutch pointed up to the roof. "Do you see those two cracked rafters? You need to scab in a piece to brace the joists. Also, the broken boards on the stalls need to be replaced. Actually any wood that is rotted or missing should be replaced."

"Well, I-I've never fixed anything like that."

"Homer can tell you how." Dutch opened a stall door with difficulty. "Better oil all the door hinges too."

"Okay," Luther sighed.

"Just spend a little time looking around and let me know what you think you'll need. Then meet me up at the house. I'm going up to speak to your friends."

Luther wandered around the barn for several minutes, realizing this was a test of sorts, but he was anxious to return to the house. He really needed Homer's help in figuring out what to tell Dutch and then he needed to write it all down. And besides, he was hungry. He hiked quickly back up to the house but couldn't find Homer or Dutch. He did run into Juniper, though, and that was better.

"I think Homer needs something to eat," he said.

"You live here now, Luther. You can help yourself to what's in the kitchen. Just be sure to tell me when something is running low before it's all gone."

"Yeah," Luther smiled, but Homer complained that the food was too healthy."

"Oh did he?" she smiled back. I'm afraid Scarlett feels the same way. How about you?"

"I'm fine. I mean, well, I like junk food too, but I'll eat most anything."

Juniper nodded. "Did Dutch talk to you about the barn?"

"Yes. He asked me to tell him what I need, but I don't really know. I could use a little bite to eat first."

Juniper stopped walking and stared at him. "You need to realize that no one is going to tell you what, when, where or why anymore. You are on your own here."

"That'll take some getting used to."

"Hunger is a great motivator." She started to leave, then stopped and turned around and managed a little smile. "Maybe we can get together later and talk." She walked off.

Luther shook his head as he went to the kitchen to forage for something tasty for Homer. He found some bread, peanut butter and honey. That seemed like a good bet for both of them. He made a couple of sandwiches and went to look for Homer. He passed the open door to Buster's room and noticed him sitting on his bed, strumming his guitar. He beamed as he knocked on Homer's door.

"Luther?" Homer asked.

"Best I could do is a peanut butter and honey sandwich," Luther said as he entered and handed Homer one of the sandwiches.

"Thanks young fella."

"Dutch gave me a job to do."

"Oh yeah? What's that?"

"Fixing up the big barn down by the road."

"That'll be quite a job."

"Do you know what he's going to do with it?" Luther asked.

"Nope," Homer replied. "But knowing Dutch, he has some big idea."

"That's pretty much what he said. He wants me to take stock of what needs to be done, but I haven't a clue really. He said you could help me figure it out."

"Sure. I'll go down and — what did the kids call it back at the circus? *Stupidvise.*"

Luther laughed. "I could use some stupidvice."

"Maybe Buster wants to join us. He could make it all go smoother with his music."

Luther smiled. "Good idea. Let's ask him." Luther and Homer went over to Buster's room and found him quite amenable to the idea. The threesome slowly traipsed down to the barn and set to making a list as Buster played his guitar.

Meanwhile, Dutch had brought Leo and Tasha into the music room. "So what's your story?" Dutch asked after Leo and Tasha had finished gushing over all the music and recording equipment, as well as the gold records hanging on the wall.

"Tasha needs a place to stay. I'm a union organizer. I was coming up here to work with the marijuana growers and workers now that it's legal."

"You're not the first. You know that."

"Yeah, but I've got more to offer."

"Well, I'm not interested in hearing your spiel. I have a good thing going, and been doing it for a lot of years."

"I see," Leo replied, recalculating his approach. "I really wasn't coming here to recruit you or anything. My friend Gordon just told me that you might be okay with letting Tasha stay here."

"And who's Gordon?"

"Luther's lawyer."

"And why does Tasha need a place to hide?"

Leo looked over at Tasha. He didn't know how much she wanted to tell Dutch, although he felt they owed him the truth. She cleared her throat. Apparently she felt the same way. "I was a dealer/call girl in Las Vegas. A pimp beat me up because I wouldn't work for him. He would probably kill me if I stayed there." She took a breath. "I have a degree in botany."

Dutch didn't react to the first part of her explanation, but when she said she had a degree in botany, his eyes lit up. "Botany, eh?"

"I also grew up on a farm."

"So you know your way around animals too?" Dutch asked.

"Yes I do."

"Welcome," Dutch smiled, extending his hand. "Let's find Juniper and she can show you a room. And what are you going to do, Leo?"

"I, uh, have some appointments around the county."

"You going to be staying here too?"

"I'd like to be able to, if that's okay."

"Are you going to need your own room?"

Uh oh. How was Leo supposed to answer that? He didn't even want to look at Tasha. He just wanted her to answer so he wouldn't have to. But she didn't. So he did, in as noncommittal a way as possible. "Whatever works best for you."

Dutch laughed heartily. "I get it. As soon as you two decide, you can let Juniper know. Come on. Let's go find her." Leo and Tasha followed Dutch out.

"Juniper?" Dutch called out as they got to the door to Juniper's room. Juniper opened the door, saw it was Dutch and left the room, closing the door behind her. She motioned them to follow her to a different room.

"This is Leo and Tasha," Dutch said after they had all gotten into the room and shut the door.

"Thanks a lot for helping us," Leo said.

"Do we have two rooms left for them?" Dutch asked.

"In the house? No. There's plenty of room in the trimmers' dorm, though. But there's only one room left in the house."

"I guess the choice has been made for you," Dutch said to Leo and Tasha.

12

LUTHER, HOMER AND BUSTER ENDED UP HAVING A GREAT TIME IN THE BARN — EVEN THOUGH LUTHER HAD TO DO ALL THE WORK. Leo and Tasha wandered around the farm, admiring the beauty and exploring all the trails and buildings. Leo knew he should have been working the phones, but couldn't resist the chance to spend the day with a content Tasha. When dusk descended, Juniper had dinner on the table and summoned them all to the kitchen.

"I make dinner every day, but you're on your own the rest of the time," she said as everyone took their food from the counter and sat down at the large kitchen table. Everyone, that is, except Scarlett, who was still in her room.

"How should we work out paying for room and board?" Leo asked.

"I don't want your money," Dutch answered. "Just your help."

"What kind of help?"

"I'll let you know."

Leo considered Dutch's vague, open-ended remark before saying to everyone and no one in particular, "I'll be leaving in the morning for the day so if you need me to pick anything up in town, let me know."

"You going to be leaving every day?" Homer asked.

"I don't know. It depends."

"Will you come back every evening?"

Leo glanced at Tasha. "I'm not sure." He looked back at Homer, waiting to find out what he wanted, but Homer just smiled.

They continued to eat in silence until Dutch finally spoke several minutes later. "Any of you have any experience with animals? Besides Homer here — before he was a farm boy up in Honeydew, he helped Noah on the Ark."

"Yep," Homer replied, rubbing his whiskers. "We almost left you donkeys behind." Laughter rippled around the table.

"Now you're getting confused with the circus," Dutch said.

"Maybe. But it's all the same to me now. Juniper here has that horse—"

"You have a horse?" Luther asked. "Where is it? There's no animal in the barn."

"I keep it on the other side of the property," Juniper answered indifferently.

"We didn't have much, being sharecroppers an' all," Buster offered, "but I know my way around chickens, ducks, turkeys. Had a goat, too."

"You already know I was a farm girl," Tasha smiled.

Dutch smiled back. "This is good."

"Why you asking?" Buster said.

"I have some plans." Dutch turned to Leo. "Could you come to the music room after dinner? I have some things I'd like to talk over with you."

"Me?" He laughed. "I grew up in New York City. The only animals I grew up around were rats, pigeons and cockroaches."

"I'm not looking to you for that kind of help." Dutch then turned to Luther. "How did the barn cleanup go?"

"Pretty good. But I'm not finished," Luther replied.

"Oh I didn't expect you to finish in one day. Do you know what you need to start the prep work?"

"What are we preparing it for?" Luther asked.

"Farm animals," laughed Buster. "Haven't you been listenin' to the conversation?"

Luther ignored Buster. "You mean the stalls and rafters?"

"Yeah. I'll come down tomorrow and we can go through it together again."

"We're gonna be having some fun!" Homer said.

"Are you sure you've only been vaping Kobain Kush?" Dutch asked dryly.

"Hehe," laughed Buster. "I was strummin' and he was dancin' . . ."

"But I did get a list of lumber and things to buy out of him," Luther interjected.

Dutch shook his head, got up and left the table. Buster and Homer started chatting about their early farm lives. Tasha joined them while Luther helped Juniper clean up the dishes and kitchen. It was almost a surreal Norman Rockwell family portrait.

"So, Leo," Dutch said as he and Leo settled into chairs in the music room. "Would you like a beer? Or a joint?"

"A beer might be nice."

"Light? Dark?"

"Whatever you're having."

Dutch smiled and opened a couple of oatmeal stouts. He handed Leo a bottle and took a swig from his own. "I'm going to get right to the point. The pot business is going through a lot of changes with legalization, as you well know. Good for your business, not so good for mine."

"Why isn't it good for yours?" Leo asked, although he knew the answer. It was one of those catch-22 situations for those who had been growing illegally for years.

"Big business trying to take over, all the licenses, taxes, rules and regulations . . . it's a nightmare. And you have to abide by the state rules as well as the county rules and they don't always mesh."

"I know all the counties have different regulations. I'm not up on all of them and they change so often. What are the maximum acres you can grow on in Humboldt?"

"Five. That isn't the problem. I've always stayed under five acres."

"Is there a number of plants specified?" Leo asked. He had taken his phone out and was taking notes on it.

"It's all the paperwork I have to do and show them. A site plan, cultivation and operations plan for both outside and inside, and that's just the beginning. Got to have a bunch of permits and documents showing I have agreements with Cal-Fire, the Department of Fish and Wildlife, the State Water Resources Control Board . . . There are environmental, zoning and structural changes that might have to be made, and that's after paying a ridiculous amount of fees. I'd have to wait for the environmental impact study and that could take up to two years. I have one of the nicest residences for trimmers anywhere, but I would have to spend tons of money just to make it ADA compliant. I could go on and on."

"Are you getting out of the business?"

"Not totally. But I'm going to grow less, just for people I know. I don't need the headaches . . . or the money. I have some other interests that I'd like to follow up on."

Leo waited for Dutch to elaborate, but he started to strum his guitar instead. Leo wasn't sure what to do, so he just sat back and enjoyed the music. When Dutch stopped playing, Leo spoke. "And what are your other interests?"

"I have two things I'd like to do. One might involve you, if you're so inclined."

"I assume the one for me does not involve farm animals?"

Dutch laughed. "Yeah, you made that clear." He played a few chords and then looked back at Leo. "Are you happy in your job?"

"Union organizing? It's better than sitting in an office or working in a factory. And at least it has some social justice value."

Dutch nodded and played some more. "Are you good at it?"

"My job?"

"Organizing."

"I suppose," Leo answered, getting a little tired of the cat and mouse game Dutch enjoyed playing.

"Would you like to organize something else?"

"Like what?"

"A music festival?"

Leo looked at him curiously. "Here on the farm? You mean, like Woodstock?"

"Not that fucking crazy," Dutch snorted. "Something small to start with. Laid back."

"Don't you think you'd need an event organizer? And someone who's more business-minded?"

"I know how to run a business and I know the music end. I think you'd be able to do the organizing."

Leo took a breath. His mind was a jumble of thoughts and emotions. "Hmm, I don't know. Like your business, unions have been going through a lot of changes through the years. The decline in membership has been huge and we've had to do much more of a sales job to get people to join. The leadership is different too. The George Meanys and Jimmy Hoffas have been replaced with kinder and gentler souls."

Dutch smiled. "Maybe that's what's needed." He went back to his guitar and Leo sat back, listened to the music, drank his beer, and contemplated the possibilities.

They both became lost in their own thoughts. After several minutes there was a knock on the door and Juniper stuck her head in.

"I'm bringing some food up to Scarlett. I'll be there a while. Luther wants to know if there's anything else he can do this evening?"

"Send him in." Luther entered warily and Dutch motioned him to another chair. "Beer?"

"Okay."

"Oatmeal stout or something lighter?"

Luther shrugged. "I don't know much about beer. Doesn't matter."

"I guess you wouldn't. Probably something lighter, then." Dutch opened a bottle of pilsner and handed it to Luther. "Take a load off. It's too dark to do anything with Homer, and we need his input on the wiring."

"Homer can do wiring, too?"

"He used to be an electrician many years ago. He can't do the work anymore, but he can tell you what to do."

"Oh, okay. So we'll need lights and stuff," Luther looked over to Leo, "unless you have bigger plans."

"Right now I just want you to get the barn ready for animals. Like I was telling Leo here, legalization has changed the pot biz. I have some new things I want to try." He then turned to Leo. "I'm going to convince Buster to perform at the festival."

"What festival?" Luther asked.

"Dutch wants to put on a music festival here on the farm."

"Cool!"

"Okay guys," Dutch interrupted. "Enough for now. We'll talk some more tomorrow."

Leo finished his beer. "Thanks. I have a lot of phone calls to make." He smiled. "To answer you — yes."

Dutch nodded. "Glad you could use a change, too." Leo got up to leave, already mentally planning his new career around Tasha.

Luther looked at his full bottle of beer. "Um, can I take this with me?"

"Sure Just remember to recycle or Juniper will give you hell." Luther gave Dutch a blank look. "Oh. There's a bin full of bottles in the kitchen. Rinse out your bottle when you're done and put it in there."

Luther went back to the now empty kitchen. He saw the bin marked recycling, and sat down at the table and took another swig of beer. He scratched his head, thinking about all that had happened since he was left on that street corner in San Francisco. He took out his phone and scrolled through his contacts. He wanted to share his excitement. "Hello, Jed? It's Luther."

13

MORNING BROKE WITH WIND AND RAIN. The clouds whipped down across the old pasture and flitted midst the trees until Luther's breath clouded out the view through the window. He wished for a cup of coffee, but didn't know how to make it. So much for being useful. He had picked up the coffee habit in prison — just something else to grab in the dining hall — and now he had to learn how to forage for himself. He walked through the silent house to the kitchen and stared at the coffee maker. He could almost see his mother standing there, pouring in water and tossing a cup full of grinds into the basket. That's how she did everything. Never used measuring cups or spoons. He knew it wasn't that easy. He pulled a bag of bread across the counter towards the toaster and soon was spreading peanut butter over crisp-soft toast. The warmth was satisfying. He chewed, thinking of ways to get Juniper to teach him a few cooking basics.

"Good morning," Tasha said as she and Leo entered the kitchen.

"Morning. Sorry, I didn't get the coffee started."

"I'll do it," Leo said. Luther felt embarrassed and watched him closely.

"Crappy day out there," Leo said. "Damn, lost count of how many spoons I put in." Leo poured the ground coffee out of the basket and slowly counted again.

"I like this weather," Tasha said. "For once my skin doesn't feel like a lizard's."

Luther chuckled. "I'm just enjoying any weather for more than one hour a day."

"I can't even imagine what that's like," Leo said. "Gordon told me what happened to you. I assume you'll be going after some compensation."

Luther sighed. "I suppose, but who knows when that will be."

Buster arrived at that moment. "Anyone seen Homer? I knocked on his door, but he didn't answer."

"He hasn't been down here in the kitchen," Luther replied. "I'll go up and see if he needs anything."

Luther knocked quietly on Homer's door. When there was no response, he opened the door and saw Homer on his bed with his eyes closed. "Homer?" He kept calling his name as he neared the bed, hoping Homer would open his eyes. When Luther got to the bed he leaned down and put his ear next to his mouth. Phew. He was breathing. Luther shook his shoulders.

"Homer? Homer?"

Finally Homer opened his eyes. "Who? What?" Homer looked anxiously around the room.

"It's Luther. You okay?"

Homer took a deep breath. "Yeah. Uh, help me up, will you young fella?"

Luther took Homer's arm and slowly pulled him into a sitting position. "Is something wrong? Do you need something?" Luther asked.

"It's okay. Sometimes this happens. It just takes me a while to get my bearings. Would you mind walking me to the head? I feel a little wobbly."

Luther took Homer's arm and walked him into the bathroom. He was definitely shaky. "I'll wait outside the door for you."

"Much appreciated."

Juniper came out of Scarlett's room and looked at him quizzically. "Waiting for Homer," Luther said.

Juniper smiled. "It's good for Homer to have you here."

"Does he always sleep so soundly and have a hard time walking when he wakes up?" Luther asked.

"Not often, but occasionally. I usually just let him sleep as long as he needs."

"Now I feel bad. I woke him up."

"I don't know which is better. Maybe he shouldn't sleep so long."

"Could it be the pot?"

Juniper shrugged. "Maybe."

Homer came out of the bathroom, holding onto the wall as he walked. "Hey beautiful," he said to Juniper.

"You want your iPod?" she asked.

"That'd be good."

"I'll get it and meet you downstairs. Do you have some kush in your room?"

"I don't know."

"I'll check." She looked at Luther. "I'll meet you in the kitchen."

Luther helped Homer down the stairs and got him seated at the table. "Morning, Homer," Leo, Tasha, and Buster said in unison.

"You been practicing that all morning?" Homer laughed.

"Do you want coffee?" Tasha asked.

"You bet," Homer answered.

"Luther?"

"Yes. Please."

Tasha poured coffee for them while Buster stood at the stove scrambling eggs. "How about some breakfast?"

Homer and Luther both answered yes and the conversation turned to how they were all going to spend the day when being outside seemed out of the question. It was finally decided that Homer and Buster would go down to the barn with Luther and figure out how to fix it up for these farm animals that Dutch was planning to bring in. Tasha wanted to see if she could use Dutch's computer to study up on botany. It had been years and she felt like her brain had turned to mush during her time in Las Vegas. Leo had a lot of phone calls to make — resigning from his job would not be easy.

Homer had a hard time keeping his hands still enough to hold the fork or the coffee cup. The others glanced at each other, all of them wanting to help, but all of them afraid to say anything. Juniper arrived, thankfully, and took over. "Here," she said as she handed Homer his pipe. He took some tokes and soon his hand stopped shaking enough to hold the fork and cup. The others looked on in astonishment.

Homer picked up on their reaction. "Pretty cool, huh?" he said.

"Amazing," Leo said.

"Are you stoned?" Tasha asked.

"Not so I can't function."

At that moment, Dutch walked in and poured some coffee. They all welcomed him with the same chorus of good morning. "We need to do this with some music tomorrow," Buster chuckled. "I'll write us a song."

"Hey, Dutch? I was wondering if I could use your computer this morning?" Tasha asked.

Dutch looked out the window. "Later. I need it now."

Tasha almost cringed. "I'll buy my own as soon as I can get to a store."

"That'd be good." Dutch left as abruptly as he entered.

Luther looked at Juniper. "Are you sure he's okay with all of us being here?"

"He has a plan for everyone, remember? He has a lot on his mind. Don't be afraid of him."

"We just feel like we're intruding," Leo said.

"Well, you're not." Juniper poured herself a cup of coffee. "Thanks for making breakfast." She left the kitchen.

Luther looked at Buster and Homer and said, "Ready? Shall we brave the storm and walk down to the barn?" Buster nodded, Homer stood up and walked steadily to the door.

"If you wait a couple of minutes, I'll give you all a ride to the barn. I have some appointments," Leo said.

"That would be great," Luther said.

"Hey Leo?" Homer asked. "If I give you some money would you buy me some food?"

"Sure," Leo grinned. "Don't they feed you enough?"

"I need some junk food! C'mon, Leo. You never smoked weed?"

Leo laughed. "Just tell me what you want."

Juniper had been waiting for them to leave before going upstairs to get Scarlett. She was sitting up in bed when Juniper opened the door, dressed but still obviously weak. "Are you hungry?" Juniper asked.

"Not really. But I am getting tired of these four walls."

They walked downstairs and went to the kitchen. "Eggs?" Juniper asked.

"I think just toast. And tea, maybe."

Juniper joined Scarlett in the simple breakfast. "I was hoping to take you for a walk today, but the weather isn't cooperating."

"I think it'll be enough just to walk around the house. I'm so sorry, Juniper."

"Please stop apologizing! Dutch wants to talk to you when you're ready."

"Oh no! Is he mad?"

"Scarlett! He's fine with your being here. Please." Juniper watched Scarlett's lip quiver and her eyes fill with tears. She hugged her. "You've been through hell. You have nothing to apologize for. You didn't bring any of this on yourself."

Scarlett picked at her toast and sipped her tea slowly. Juniper cleaned up the kitchen while she waited. "I'm still not very hungry, I'm afraid," Scarlett said as she put her plate in the sink.

Juniper washed the plate. "Let's go find Dutch. You can take your tea with you." She took Scarlett to the music room and knocked.

"Who is it?" Dutch asked.

"Juniper and Scarlett."

"Come in." The women walked in and Juniper showed Scarlett where to sit. "How are you feeling?" Dutch asked.

"Better, I guess," Scarlett answered. "I really appreciate you letting me stay here."

"A friend of Juniper's is a friend of mine. Do you want to stay here after you get your strength back?"

Scarlett looked at Juniper when she answered. "I have nowhere else to go."

"Then you can stay."

"I want to help pay my way somehow."

"I'll find something for you to do."

"I don't have any skills." Scarlett looked at Juniper again.

"Dutch knows about your past," Juniper told her. Scarlett nodded and smiled feebly at Dutch.

"Working on a farm isn't so hard. I'm sure there's plenty you can do to help," Dutch said.

"I want to if someone will teach me."

"Then someone will."

"He's a kind, generous man," Scarlett said as they walked down the hall.

"Dutch is pretty special."

"Can I go lie down? I'm sorry—oops, there I go again."

Juniper smiled. "Sure. Do you want me to walk you to your room?"

"No. I need to start doing things on my own." Juniper nodded and started to walk away. "I love you Juniper!" Scarlett called after her.

14

THE TRIO DOWN AT THE BARN WAS NOT GETTING MUCH WORK DONE. Luther tried to get Homer's advice on how to rehab the barn for animals, but Buster kept Homer laughing and dancing.

"Hey, is it time for lunch yet?" Buster asked when he paused briefly from playing his guitar.

"I don't know," Luther replied.

"You got one of them phones, don't you?"

"Oh, yeah." Luther looked at his phone. "It's almost noon."

"Is it still raining?" Homer asked.

Luther opened the big door and peered out. "Yeah. It might be too muddy for you to walk back, Homer. I don't want you to slip."

"Hey, we could always take a nap in the hayloft? It'd be like when we were kids," Homer said to Buster.

"Is there hay up there?" Buster asked.

"I'll go look," Luther answered. He climbed up the ladder. "There is some, but are you going to be able to climb this ladder, Homer?"

"I don't know. Haven't climbed a ladder in years."

"Hey, maybe there's some hay in one of these stalls," Buster said. He looked into a couple. "I bet we could pile up the straw in these stalls for you, Homer."

"Make sure it's clean," Luther called out as he climbed down.

"Ha! Any manure in this hay got to have disintegrated by now. I doubt there's been any animals in here for ages," Homer said.

"Hey, here's a bale of hay that hasn't been cut open. That ought to be clean," Buster said.

Buster and Luther got to work and soon there was a nice nest of hay in the corner of one of the stalls. "Come on in, Homer," Luther said as he helped him up. Homer had started trembling again after Buster's music stopped. Luther wished he had thought to take some of the Kobain Kush with him when they left the house.

"You gonna sing me a lullaby, Buster?" Homer chuckled.

Buster picked up his guitar and started singing Keb' Mo's "Lullaby Baby Blues" and

Homer was asleep in no time. Buster put his guitar down and approached Luther who had busied himself in what he assumed had been the tack room with all the hooks on the wall. "You know what you're doing, young fella?"

"What do you mean?"

"You're supposed to repair this place and get it ready for animals?" Buster asked.

"That's what Dutch said."

"And do you know how to do that?"

"Not really. Homer supposedly does."

Buster smiled. "Let's get to work." Luther watched Buster take a measuring tape out of his pocket. "You got a piece of paper and a pencil?"

"No. I didn't think to bring them."

"Send yourself a text with these measurements."

"You can do that?"

Buster shook his head and smiled at Luther. "You got a lot to learn, boy, don't ya."

Luther smiled back sheepishly. "Twenty years in the slammer will do that." Luther typed as fast as he could, which wasn't very fast, while Buster measured and barked lists of things to buy. They kept at it for more than an hour until they were interrupted by Dutch's arrival.

"Where's Homer?" Dutch asked. Buster pointed to the stall where Homer was asleep in the hay.

"I sang him 'Lullaby Baby Blues.'"

Dutch smiled. "Did Homer help you, Luther?"

"No, but Buster did."

"I didn't know you had construction skills."

"I'm an old man. I've got a lot of skills," Buster answered with a twinkle in his eye.

"I have a list of stuff that Buster says we need," Luther added.

"Can I have it? I'm going into town. I'll pick up whatever I can find in Garberville, but I might have to get most of it when I go to Eureka."

"It's on my phone. I texted it to myself."

"Then text it to me. You have my number?"

"No. Just Juniper's."

"Give me your phone." Luther handed it to Dutch who added his contact info. "There you go," Dutch said as he handed it back. "I'll see you guys later." Dutch left.

"We should have asked to go with him," Buster said. "Can't enjoy the outdoors in this weather. Wouldn't have minded a little diversion."

Luther shrugged. "From what I saw of the town, there's not much diversion there. Maybe we can go to Eureka with him when he goes."

"You think living on this farm is gonna be hard?"

"Nope," Luther answered a little too quickly.

"Well, nobody's holding a gun to our heads. We can leave whenever we want."

"Is it lunchtime?" Homer called out in a shaky voice.

Luther scurried over to help Homer up. "You want me to bring you lunch. And maybe your pipe? It's still kind of wet out there."

"Are we staying here all day?"

"I am. I don't know what you want to do," Luther replied.

"I don't mind. You need help, right?"

"Buster and I did some measurements and stuff while you were sleeping. Maybe you could look things over too." Luther glanced at Buster, hoping he understood that it wasn't a matter of trusting Buster's advice, but rather giving Homer some recognition. Buster nodded.

"Why don't you trek on back to the house and get us some food and stuff. I'll stay here with Homer."

Luther was soaking wet when he got back to the house. He went upstairs to change and soon realized that he was going to have to supplement his wardrobe or he'd be doing laundry every other day. He didn't have any clean clothes to change into. Oh well. He'd only be getting wet again when he trudged back to the barn. He searched Homer's room and found the vape pen. Luckily it was full. He hadn't learned how to use it, but he had noticed how it looked when it was ready for Homer to use. He found Tasha in the kitchen making a sandwich. "Hi Luther. I could make you one of these too."

"I need three. Homer and Buster are down at the barn and I was elected to be the one who gets wet."

Tasha nodded. "Looks like you did a good job of it." She busied herself making the sandwiches. "How are you going to bring these down there without them getting soaked?"

"Good question."

"There must be some plastic bags around here," Tasha said as she pulled open drawer after drawer. She found none. "Juniper really is a fanatic, isn't she?" She went back a few drawers and found a roll of waxed paper. "Well, I'll wrap you a few presents." In a minute she had a neat stack finished. "I think that would make my great grandma proud."

"Thanks a lot Tasha. That's two meals you've made for me today."

"I'm just happy to have mundane tasks like these to do. A lot better than what I was doing before."

"What was that?" Luther asked.

"Casino dealer and call girl."

Luther blinked with surprise. She certainly came out with that easily enough. "Well . . . maybe you can get a job at a Subway."

Tasha laughed. "I think I have higher hopes than that. I'm thinking about taking some more botany courses and getting back on board with that. How about you? What do you want to do?"

"Right now, just stay here and relish my freedom."

"I feel the same way, actually. This is a perfect opportunity to do that without having to look over our shoulders. Well, I'm going to go back to the computer. Dutch is in town for a couple of hours so he said I can use it while he's gone."

Luther realized just then that he hadn't texted Dutch the notes he had made about what to buy. "Oh crap!" He took out his phone and opened the text to himself. "Hey, before you leave, could you show me how I can forward a text?"

"Sure." She took the phone. "This one?"

"Yeah. I need to copy it or something and send it to Dutch. He put his contact information in the phone for me." Tasha did it so fast that Luther didn't get a chance to see what she was doing. He'd ask Juniper to show him how later.

He got to the barn and distributed the sandwiches. "Nothing to drink?" Buster asked.

"Sorry, I didn't think of it."

Buster walked over to a hose and turned it on, but nothing came out. "Shit! Gonna have to check the water situation out too." After lunch Homer vaped while Buster picked his guitar and once again, Luther was left doing all the work. But like Tasha, he didn't mind doing mundane tasks.

When they all gathered around the kitchen table that night for dinner, there were eight. Scarlett had finally joined them. Dutch had done a large grocery shopping and Juniper had consented to buying meat, so she had made hamburgers for those that wanted them. It was heartening to watch Homer scarf down two of them and a shaking hand did not deter him. The conversation grew lively and relaxed as this group of strangers slowly morphed into a family of sorts.

Dutch and Buster went to the music room to jam after dinner. Leo and Homer joined them, while Tasha took Scarlett to her room. Juniper and Luther were left to clean up the kitchen and wash dishes.

"How's everything going in the barn?"

"Fine. Looks like Tasha might help you with Scarlett."

"Scarlett's not a problem for me!" Juniper scowled.

"Sorry. I didn't mean it that way."

Juniper sighed. "I'm sorry too. It has been really hard, but it seems that the worst is over."

Luther tried steering the conversation towards Juniper. "So what are you going to do without the trimmers here?"

"As you've heard, Dutch has some big ideas."

"How does that involve you?"

"He wants to focus on that and leave me totally in charge of the pot growing operation."

"Oh, I didn't realize."

"It'll be on a smaller scale than it's been, but it's still a lot of work by myself."

"By yourself?"

"Yeah, that and the gardening."

"Tasha told me that she has a degree in botany. Maybe she can help you."

"That would be nice."

"She said she wanted to get back into that. Did you know she used to be a casino dealer and prostitute?"

"No." Juniper looked off into space.

"I can help you too," Luther added.

Juniper smiled at him. "I think Dutch has other plans for you. I'm afraid you're the one young workhorse around here."

Luther smiled back. "Leo's not so old."

"Right now, Dutch just wants you to get the barn ready for animals."

"Why does he want the animals here? Just for milk and eggs?"

Juniper smiled. "Dutch will let you know his plans when he's ready."

"Okay. If you don't want to talk about animals, how about talking about you?"

"You and I are alike, Luther. We are private people who don't like to talk about our pasts."

"Yeah, but I have a good reason. I'm just wondering what yours is."

Juniper took a breath and stared at Luther for a moment. She finally spoke. "Crappy family and foster homes until I was eighteen."

"Were you and Dutch ever a couple?"

"No. I think that's enough prying."

"Fair enough."

Juniper looked into Luther's eyes and smiled. "Do you really want to live out here in the boonies? Or is it just somewhere to go? I mean, don't you kind of want to experience more and see more places?"

"Maybe at some point, but I like it here. And I like the people here." He inhaled. "I like you."

Juniper didn't answer right away and Luther felt like an idiot for saying anything. She started to leave and Luther felt even worse. "Let's go upstairs to my room."

Luther exhaled. "Oh man, I was so afraid—"

"Just come on," Juniper smiled.

When they got to Juniper's room and closed the door, Luther said softly, "You realize I haven't — you know — for twenty years. And not ever with a woman. Just fooled around with a girl or two."

"It's not rocket science," Juniper said and then kissed him.

15

THE NEXT DAY WAS BRIGHT AND SUNNY. Leo and Tasha were the first ones up. "What exactly does Dutch want you to do?" Tasha asked as they waited for the coffee to brew.

"I'm not sure. He wants to have a music festival here. I don't know the first thing about event planning, but Dutch seems to think I can do it."

"I'm sure you can, but why does he want to do that? He said himself he doesn't need money. And does he really want to bring people to the farm who might rip him off?"

"I imagine he's thought about all that."

"Yeah, you're probably right."

"What about you?" Leo asked.

"What do you mean?"

"What were you looking up on Dutch's computer?"

"Botany classes. But I need my own computer. I can't always borrow Dutch's."

"Are you sticking to botany?" Leo asked.

"To start. We'll see where it leads. What about your apartment?" Tasha asked with raised eyebrows.

"I haven't decided what to do about that."

Luther and Juniper entered the kitchen at that moment putting an end to the conversation. "Thanks for tending to Scarlett last night," Juniper said to Tasha.

"There really wasn't any tending. She seems to be doing fine. Just a little sad. I'd like to talk with her. I think I can help."

Juniper shrugged. "If she's open to it, go right ahead."

Dutch entered and everyone voiced their customary good mornings as he poured his coffee. "Hey Leo, when are you going to be finished wrapping up your union business?" Dutch asked.

"It'll probably take at least a couple of weeks, maybe more like a month."

Dutch nodded and turned to Luther. "Can I see you a minute?" Luther reluctantly followed him out. He wasn't ready to face the mundane tasks at the barn. He was much more interested in staying with Juniper in the kitchen and reflecting on the previous night.

"What's up?" Luther asked as they sat down in the music room.

"Did you drive before you were incarcerated?"

"Yeah, but I didn't have a car so not much."

"You need to get a license. I need you to be able to drive."

"Okay. Uh, I might need a couple of refresher lessons."

"Ask Juniper." Luther's face lit up. "You can use the pickup."

"Might take a little longer. I've never driven a stick."

"I'll bring the stuff I bought down to the barn in about an hour."

"Okay. I'll be there." Luther waited but when Dutch didn't say anymore, he got up and went back to the kitchen. Juniper was stirring a pot. Tasha and Leo were gone, and Luther hoped that Buster and Homer would sleep in. "Dutch wants you to teach me how to drive the pickup."

"You don't know how to drive?"

"Well, I don't know how to drive a stick."

Juniper smiled. "Then I guess that's something else you'll need to practice. Do you want some oatmeal?" Juniper noticed Luther's crestfallen face. "I didn't mean that the way it sounded. I wasn't faking anything last night. I look forward to practicing with you." She kissed him. "I'm going to bring some oatmeal up to Homer. If he hasn't come down by this time, it's usually a sign that he needs to stay in bed, at least for the morning."

"Does he see a doctor?" Luther asked.

"He won't."

"Shouldn't he?"

Juniper shrugged. "Not my call." She put some oatmeal in a bowl and took a spoon out of the drawer. She put it on a tray with a mug of coffee. "Help yourself." She left before Luther could arrange with her for a driving lesson or ask her for help with his phone.

Buster made his presence known with a booming hello and a slap on Luther's back. "Hey Buster," Luther answered. "There's oatmeal if you want it. And coffee."

"Thanks, buddy. What's on tap for today? More barn work?"

"That and Juniper's going to teach me how to drive a stick. Dutch wants me to get a license."

"That'd be a good thing. Then you can take me and Homer to town for some better food."

"You don't like Juniper and Dutch's choices either?"

"I don't feel like Homer. But it would be nice to choose and do some of my own cooking."

"Are you coming down to the barn with me today? Homer's still in bed."

"I'll meander down in a while. Dutch wants to talk to me this morning," Buster replied.

"He's bringing the stuff we told him to buy down to the barn."

"Alright. I'll come down with you." They finished eating and put their bowls and coffee mugs in the sink. They started to leave when Luther turned back and washed the dishes. "Well, aren't you the perfect guest," Buster chuckled.

"My mom taught me well." They ambled down to the barn, watching for Dutch's truck. Although the sun was out, the weather was getting cooler and they knew the rains would be coming more and more frequently as winter approached. They might as well enjoy the outdoors while they could.

They had done just about all there was to do preparing for the repairs and construction and were sitting outside, shooting the breeze, when Dutch arrived. Luther jumped up, embarrassed that Dutch might think he was being lazy. Buster laughed at him and didn't budge. Dutch dropped the tailgate and Luther sprang into action, helping Dutch unload the truck. Buster finally got up and joined in. "I think I got everything you asked for," Dutch said as they brought in the last of it. "Let me know if you need anything else," he added and then drove off.

Juniper showed up with Homer about one. "Brought you lunch." She turned to Luther. "I thought we'd have our first practice session about four." She smiled. "That would be driving lesson." Luther returned the smile.

"How you feeling, Homer?" Luther asked after Juniper left.

"Hasn't been a good day. Dutch mixed me up some new-fangled mixture of marijuana and that helped, but it makes my head much fuzzier."

"Maybe you should go to the doctor," Luther replied.

"No. They don't help. They just give me more medicine that has worse side effects than what Dutch gives me." He smiled. "Just got to keep the music going."

"I didn't bring my guitar today." Buster said.

"No need. I got my iPod."

The trio kept busy all afternoon and soon Juniper showed up. "Is it four o'clock already?" Luther asked.

"Yep. I'm going to drive Homer back up to the house. You want a ride too, Buster?"

"You bet."

Juniper left with the two men while Luther tidied up a bit. He was waiting outside when Juniper returned. "Get in and let's go," she said as she got out of the driver's side and walked around the truck to the passenger side.

Luther took a breath and climbed in nervously. "I really do need a refresher course."

"Do you know anything at all about driving a stick?"

"I know there's a clutch and a gear shift. That's about it."

"Do you know what they do?"

"Not really."

"Lesson number one, then, is that you need to step on the clutch in order to change gears." She smiled at him affectionately, but Luther wasn't sure there wasn't a trace of teasing there too. "Now rev the motor," Juniper continued. "You have to spin it more than necessary at first until you get the hang of engaging the gears or you'll stall the motor." Luther round the motor up to a whine. "Now, let the clutch out slowly." He did — or thought he did. The truck leaped forward — almost strangling Juniper against her seat belt — and then stalled. "Well, that wasn't quite the same way you took my breath away last night," Juniper gasped.

"Don't distract me!"

"Okay, try again."

Luther managed a herky-jerky take off the second time, stalled again on the third time, and by the fifth time managed a fairly respectable, if noisy, take off. "Hey!" grinned Luther.

"Now shift into second." Luther did this without a hitch. "It's a lot easier, isn't it?"

"Uh huh."

"Third. This will make you more relaxed about attempting first again." Luther smiled as the truck picked up speed. "Now stop!" Luther stepped on the brake firmly and the truck ground to a halt. The motor started shaking. "Clutch in! Clutch in or you'll stall the motor!"

He jabbed in the clutch. "Was I supposed to shift down to second?" he asked as the motor picked up to a relaxed idle.

"No, not unless you're going down to Shelter Cove." Luther glanced at her. "Downshifting saves your brakes going down long, winding grades. Or gives you more power to climb."

"How will I know when to do that?"

"Practice. Basically, if you give the truck a little more gas when climbing and it doesn't respond, it needs to be downshifted. You'll eventually figure out that the gears move you more smoothly and economically than just using the gas pedal. When you upshift under average acceleration and the truck suddenly feels free when the clutch is depressed, you've waited too long to shift up. You've just wasted gas going nowhere."

"So much to think about," Luther sighed.

"Don't worry about it. You can already get the truck rolling and that's the hard part.

Practice will make everything second nature. Most of the time." Luther looked over at her. "Yes, even I screw up once in awhile."

"So we'll need to practice," Luther replied, leaning into her. "A lot."

"Get your motor running," Juniper said coolly, pushing back against him. Luther revved the motor, popped the clutch, and stalled the truck. "Again," she sighed. This time he started off smoothly, with the motor hardly protesting at all. "Now through the gate."

"Really?"

"Relax. All you'll run into are a few pot heads and deer."

Not reassuring. I've never really driven on roads like this before."

"I'll take curves and potheads over crosswalks and assholes anytime," she answered.

They spent another half hour driving the country roads that surrounded the farm without serious mishap and even a bit of relaxed laughter between the two of them. Luther felt great when they pulled up to the house. "Maybe tomorrow we can go into town so I can practice there a bit and then I'll make an appointment for my license."

"I've got to get dinner started," Juniper said distractedly as she looked for her purse.

"I'll shower and be down to help you." He instinctively leaned over to kiss her, but she pulled away.

"I don't want the others to know about us."

"I think they already do."

"Well, we don't have to be obvious about it," she said as she slid out of the seat and slammed the door. Luther's sunny mood soured. He went upstairs and ended up staying in his room until dinner was ready.

16

EVERYONE WAS LOST IN THEIR OWN THOUGHTS DURING DINNER, WITH ONLY THE SOFT CLATTER OF SILVERWARE AND GLASSES BREAKING THE SILENCE. After they ate Dutch and Leo left for the music room, Homer and Buster went back to their own rooms, and Tasha took Scarlett back to her room, leaving Juniper and Luther to clean up. "Does Dutch ever leave the farm?" Luther asked.

"During winter after the harvest is done and the buds are trimmed."

"And you?"

Juniper shrugged. "I spent many years on the road. I kind of like staying put for now. It's nice to have a home."

Luther nodded in agreement. "Is there a washing machine here?"

"Yeah." Juniper smiled. "Do I need to show you how to use it?"

Luther nodded. "Afraid so. I really need to get to town and get some more clothes."

"Do you have any money to buy them?"

"Not really."

"Sometimes the trimmers leave stuff here. Let me look in their dorm and see if there's something there." She started to leave and Luther stood, not sure if he was supposed to follow. "Come on. I'll show you where the trimmers stay."

They walked outside and were immediately accosted by a hound dog. The dog barked incessantly, making Luther wary, but Juniper spoke softly to it and held out her hand for the dog to sniff. "What's wrong, puppy?" she said as she gently put her hand on its head and started to scratch behind its ears. The dog turned its barking into a whine. Juniper stopped petting the dog and sniffed the air. "Do you smell smoke?"

Luther sniffed. "Yeah. Is something burning on the farm?" Luther asked, looking around.

"Maybe that's what this pup is trying to tell us. Let's follow and see if —" she picked up the dog's tail —"if she leads us."

The dog started running away from the house and past the trimmers' quarters. Luther and Juniper followed, but the dog was too fast so she had to keep running back to them to see that they were indeed coming. The smell of smoke got stronger and stronger the further they ran. "Shouldn't we call 911 or something?" Luther asked.

"Sure, but where will we tell them to send the fire truck?"

"I don't know, but we shouldn't waste any time." Luther took out his phone and dialed. "There's a fire somewhere. We smell the smoke but don't know where it is." He paused, listening to the operator and then turned to Juniper. "They know. Fire trucks are on the way." He talked back into the phone. "Okay. Thanks." He put his phone away.

"Where did the operator say the fire is?"

"North of town is all she said."

"Crap. We're north of town. We better get back to the house and see if we can find out more info," Juniper said as she turned back. We need to let the others know in case we have to evacuate." Luther followed, and much to their surprise, so did the dog.

They ran inside and Luther asked, "How will we find out where the fire is?"

"You go upstairs and tell everyone to come down. I'll tell Dutch. Then we can see if there's any news on TV."

"There's a TV here?"

Juniper shook her head. "We're not total hermits, you know. It's in the living room."

"Where's the living room?"

"Just go get everyone and tell them to meet us in the kitchen." Juniper ran toward the back of the house while Luther raced upstairs. The dog looked at them both as if choosing who to follow, but decided on Juniper when she called out, "Come on, pup."

Luther knocked loudly on all the bedrooms doors shouting, "Everyone needs to come downstairs to the kitchen now!"

Buster opened his door with guitar in hand, "What's going on?"

"Is Homer with you?"

"No, he's in his room."

"Please get him and come down. There's a fire somewhere and it might be close by."

Tasha and Scarlett came out of Tasha's room at that moment. "Where's the fire?" Tasha asked.

"We're not sure. Just come to the kitchen." Luther started to run back downstairs, but thought maybe he needed to help Buster with Homer. He turned around and entered Homer's room just as Buster was helping him out of bed. Luther grabbed Homer's other arm and pulled him up. "Can you walk okay?"

"Yeah, yeah. But bring my vape pipe would you? It's full, I think."

Luther grabbed the pipe off Homer's night table and also grabbed his iPod. "Buster, you'd better bring your guitar in case we have to evacuate."

"What the hell?" Buster grumbled.

Luther called out to Tasha and Scarlett. "You might bring anything you want to hang on to in case we have to leave."

They all scurried around. Luther ran to his room, but he had absolutely nothing he needed other than his phone. "Come on Homer. Let's go."

Juniper was on the phone when they all got to the kitchen. "Yes, okay, thanks. She hung up. C'mon, let's turn on the news. It's still quite a few miles away but it's moving fast. I'll take you where the TV is and then I need to help Dutch."

The dog followed the group. "Where did the beautiful pup come from?" Tasha asked as they walked through the hall.

"She came to us barking, trying to tell us something. That's when we smelled the smoke," Luther said.

Juniper opened some French doors to another large, gorgeous room with floor to ceiling windows and more beautiful artwork. Everyone sank into the overstuffed furniture and the dog jumped up next to Scarlett, nuzzling her as if she was her long-lost owner. "Hi sweet pup. Where's your home?" Scarlett asked as she petted and hugged the dog.

Juniper turned on the TV and found that all the Eureka stations were covering what they were calling the Bull Creek Fire.

"Where's Bull Creek?" Luther asked.

"It's in the Humboldt Redwood State Park northwest of us. Some of the oldest coastal redwoods are there in the Rockefeller Grove."

"It would be awful if they burned," Tasha lamented.

"Redwood trees don't easily burn, especially old ones," Homer said. "They usually just get scorched and sprout again."

"Oh, right," Tasha sighed, annoyed that she hadn't remembered.

"Hey, you wouldn't know that coming from Illinois," Leo murmured.

"Someone with a degree in botany should know that," she answered.

"Dutch and I have to get some stuff together," Juniper cut in, "so watch to see what they're saying about evacuating." She left and Luther turned up the volume.

Juniper and Dutch filled a large suitcase with important papers and valuables including thumb drives and his personal favorite memorabilia. They hoped there would be enough time to load up all the cars and trucks with the instruments, the computer, the safes and the trimmed marijuana buds that were ready to sell. "They're all in the living room watching

TV," Juniper said. "Tasha and I can drive cars, Luther can drive the truck, Leo can drive his car and you can drive yours."

"How's Luther doing with the driving?" Dutch asked.

"Good enough for an emergency. I'd better go to the living room and see what the news said." Her phone suddenly beeped with a text from the Humboldt County Emergency Alert system. "It's just a warning. We're not even in voluntary evacuation yet."

"We better be ready to go anytime just the same."

She nodded and hurried off. "Do you have your valuables?" she asked the group as she rushed into the living room.

"I made sure they got them," Luther answered.

"Okay. We need to be prepared. Tasha, you drive right?"

"Yes."

"We need to load up the cars and truck so we can leave quickly if we need to. Leo and Luther, Dutch needs you to help him. Tasha please come with me. Buster, take care of Homer and Scarlett. Homer, are you walking okay tonight?"

"I'm walking fine."

"I'm strong enough to help," Scarlett said.

"Okay," Juniper answered. "Follow me."

"Us too?" Buster asked.

"You and Homer stay here and watch the news for new developments."

Luther, Leo, Tasha and Scarlett followed Juniper outside. She threw the keys to one of the cars to Tasha and the truck to Luther. "Are we leaving?" Luther asked.

"Not until we have to. But we need to load up the vehicles. Tasha, you and Scarlett come with me. Luther, you need to pack the back of the pickup with the product. Leo, go to the music room and help Dutch."

"The product?" Luther asked.

"The buds . . . the pot that's manicured and ready to sell. C'mon. I'll show you where and then you can drive the truck over. Just a sec, Tasha and Scarlett, I'll be right with you."

Luther marveled at how Juniper was taking charge. He grinned at her. "You amaze me!"

"No time for sweet talk!" She brought him to a small building made of cement blocks and watched as she punched a keypad to some kind of alarm system before unlocking the door. He peered inside and saw stacks of plastic bins. "Do you need help?" Juniper asked. "Maybe I should send Scarlett down. They're not too heavy."

"I can do it. Let her help you and Tasha." Juniper jogged off and Luther went to get the truck, a little apprehensive about driving without Juniper sitting next to him, but glad, on the other hand, that she wouldn't be there to see him fumble.

Juniper took a detour into the living room before rejoining Tasha and Scarlett outside. "Is there anything new?" she asked breathlessly.

"It says the fire is moving swiftly toward Redwood Road," Buster replied.

"Shit!" Juniper exclaimed.

"Is that close?" Homer asked.

"I don't know. Maybe about three miles."

"Uh oh. What should we do?" Homer replied.

"Did they say where they were evacuating?"

"North of it. Are we north?" Buster asked.

"No. We're south of Redwood. Keep watching the TV." She ran out to find Dutch as she called out to Tasha and Scarlett, "Load the boxes and suitcases that are in the hallway!"

Dutch came out of his music room. "What's going on?"

"They're evacuating north of Redwood Road. We're loading up the cars and truck now. But where should we go?" Juniper asked.

"Let me make a couple of phone calls."

Juniper ran throughout the house to look around and make sure she hadn't forgotten anything important. Tasha rushed in. "What else should we take? There's still some room."

"Don't forget to leave room for people to sit."

"And the dog," Tasha added.

"Oh man, I forgot about her." Juniper smiled.

"Are we leaving as soon as we're packed?" Tasha asked.

"Not yet. The fire is still at least three miles away and we're not in mandatory evacuation yet. Help me with this box. It's heavy."

The two women lugged the box outside and put it in the car that still had enough room in the trunk. "I think we've filled up as much as we can," Tasha said.

"Let's go see if Luther needs any help."

The three women and the dog ran to the truck. "Look!" Luther shouted to them and pointed to the north toward a red glow.

"Wow!" Scarlett and Tasha said in unison.

"Shit! The fire's come over Bear Buttes. It's definitely getting closer." She turned toward Scarlett and Tasha. "Go help Luther. I've got to tell Dutch and get Buster and Homer." Juniper hurried back to the house.

17

THE DULL RED GLOW IN THE SKY SLOWLY GREW BRIGHTER UNTIL FLAMES OUTLINED A WAVERING, SMOKY RIDGELINE. Scarlett, Tasha and Luther watched, mesmerized. The dog, constantly watching the shadows, started whining and then barking, as something leaped out of the darkness. Scarlett let out a startled little scream as a singed calico cat landed on her shoulders, claws out. "Ow!" Scarlett laughed, pulling the cat off her shoulders and cuddling it against her chest. The dog continued barking at the cat. "Oh, shush Gypsy dog. No need to be jealous."

"Gypsy dog?" Tasha asked, laughing at the spectacle she just witnessed.

"I thought it was an appropriate name for this beautiful hound."

Scarlett turned to Luther. "Does this cat belong to Dutch?"

Luther shrugged. "No idea. I've never seen it."

"She's petrified."

"Probably of the dog," Tasha said.

"Or the fire," Scarlett replied. "Look at her fur."

"You must have some special way with animals," Luther said. Scarlett smiled as she cooed at the cat and petted the dog.

"Are there any more bins that have to be loaded into the truck?" Tasha asked.

"A few." Luther said.

"Do you need help?" Scarlett called out as Tasha and Luther ran off.

"Stay with the animals," Luther shouted back.

Meanwhile Juniper found Buster and Homer slumped on the sofa. "Any news?" she said breathlessly.

"Nope. Just to be prepared to evacuate. Where are we gonna go, anyway?" Homer asked.

"I don't know yet. Dutch is making some calls, but we'll probably just drive over to Garberville and see what happens. Do they say the roads are clear?"

"I think so. Haven't said they're not."

"Are you feeling okay, Homer?"

"I took a little off the pipe. But will I have enough if I need more?"

"I packed the stash Dutch has for you. It's in the car."

Homer patted Juniper's arm. "You're an angel, thinking of me through all this."

"Hey what happened to that dog?" Buster asked.

"She's with Scarlett. You guys okay to just sit tight here for now?"

Buster and Homer nodded. Buster had taken out his guitar and was picking a tune. "We're doing just fine," Buster answered.

Juniper decided to take one more quick walk around the whole house to see if she'd forgotten anything important when Dutch approached her. "I'm having a hard time reaching some people. I guess everyone's busy packing up their stuff. Where's the fire now?" Dutch asked.

"Last I heard it's just over the Buttes, but the wind is coming out of the north so we are in the path."

"Hopefully the wind will shift. We'll just drive south. I'll still try to reach some friends of mine who live far enough from the fire and may have space for the bins."

Juniper went back outside. The smoke was now making it hard to breathe and she worried about Homer's ability to withstand it. She blinked her stinging eyes and saw Scarlett coming towards her with something in her arms. "Who's that?"

"Minnie. Isn't she beautiful?"

Luther drove up in the truck. "All packed and ready to go," he said as he climbed out.

Buster came outside. "Holy shit!" they heard Buster cry out in the dark. "It's smoky out here."

"Is something wrong?" Juniper called out.

Buster appeared through the smoke. "Homer's fretting."

"About what?"

"Not sure. His words are kind of slurred."

"Did he finish vaping what was left?"

"I think so. I wasn't sure what to do."

"I'll go," Luther said as he rushed inside. He found Homer asleep on the sofa. "Homer? Wake up." He shook his shoulders to no avail. "Homer!" Luther looked around for the vape pipe and found it on the side table. It was empty. He turned back to Homer and shook him more forcefully, but still no response. He leaned down, putting his ear next to Homer's mouth and listened for breathing. It was shallow, but there. He ran back outside. "He won't wake up!" he exclaimed.

"It happens sometimes," Juniper replied. "Let him sleep. It's probably best right now."

"So what do we do now? Just stand around and wait?" Tasha asked.

"Maybe we should wait inside. At least it isn't hard to breathe in there," Luther said.

"I agree," Buster said as he turned back toward the door. They all filed in with Scarlett carrying the cat, and Gypsy tagging behind her.

They returned to where they had sat earlier, but this time Tasha made a beeline for the seat next to Scarlett. "Ha! Beat you to it, Gypsy."

"Maybe I should give Minnie and Gypsy some food and water," Scarlett murmured.

"Minnie?" Tasha asked.

"That's what I named the cat."

"I'm rather hungry myself," Buster said.

"Dammit," Juniper sighed. "I forgot to pack food and water."

"Luther, give me a hand," Tasha said. "Let's get everyone something to eat. At least we can have full stomachs before we leave, if we have to."

"I'll help." Juniper started to stand.

"You've been running around like crazy," Tasha replied. "Sit down. Luther and I will do it. You need a break."

Juniper smiled. "Yeah. I do." The TV announcer paused to read his teleprompter. "Breaking news. The evacuation order has expanded to include the Salmon Creek area.

Those living near Grenz Lane, Pine Drive and Thomas Road are ordered to leave now."

"Is that near us?" Buster asked no one in particular.

"It's northwest of us," Juniper explained.

"Are we okay?"

"For now."

"What are we gonna do about Homer?" Buster asked.

"Let's try to get him up when they get back with the food. Maybe that will help. I could get him some more pot, but I'd rather wait if he can. Dutch will know what strain would be better for him in this condition."

Tasha and Luther arrived with a large spread of crackers and cheese and a bottle of wine. "I hope it's okay, Juniper," Tasha said as she took out the cork. "We found this in the cupboard. Thought it might help us get through the night."

"Pour me a glass!" laughed Juniper.

Luther put two bowls on the floor and filled them with water from a jug. Gypsy immediately started lapping it up and Minnie jumped down to drink from the other bowl. The others took wine, water, bread and cheese and silently watched the news reports as they ate. Homer finally opened his eyes and Luther jumped up to get him some water. "Thanks pal," Homer said as he sipped.

"Are you okay?" Luther asked.

"I think I just needed some shuteye." Homer's words were clear and they all breathed a sigh of relief.

Dutch and Leo joined them but there wasn't much conversation for the next hour or so as they sat watching the television. "Seems like Minnie and Gypsy have mended any bad feelings between them," Luther commented as he glanced at Scarlett, sleeping with the cat on her lap and the dog at her feet.

"Probably just happy to be rescued," Tasha replied.

Juniper jumped up. "Oh my God! I need to go check on Zorba!"

"Zorba?" the others asked in unison.

"My horse. He's probably terrified!" Juniper rushed out, grabbing one of the flashlights used to go between buildings after dark.

Luther ran after her. "Wait, I'll go with you." He caught up to her and instinctively grabbed her hand. Surprisingly, Juniper did not let go. "Where is he?"

"Probably out by the pond. That's his usual hangout."

"Does he have a barn?"

"No, just a covered lean-to for when it rains." They reached the pond, but Zorba was nowhere to be found. They did see several deer drinking from the pond and heard the howls of coyotes.

"They sure sound creepy," Luther muttered.

"City slicker!" Juniper punched him lightly on the arm. "C'mon, let's see if Zorba's in his house." She pulled him through some trees to a three-sided shed. Zorba was, in fact, standing inside. "There he is!" Juniper ran up to him and Luther watched, smiling, as they nuzzled each other.

"He sure looks happy to see you."

"He's shaking."

Luther shivered himself. "I don't blame him." He heard a rustling sound and flashed his light directly into big, round eyes that seemed to be a reddish color with no pupils. As he moved the flashlight upwards, he noticed the large antlers and concluded there was a huge buck staring at him. "Uh, Juniper? Look here."

Juniper watched as Luther moved the flashlight beam from her to the buck. "Wow. That's a huge stag!" she exclaimed.

"Is he gonna come after us?"

"He's more afraid of us than we are of him." The stag pranced around, pawing the ground. "The fire has him all agitated."

Luther shouted and pointed the flashlight in the other direction. "Look there!"

"Hey, don't yell. You'll freak us all out."

The flashlight revealed eyes of green and yellow. "What are those?" As he moved the beam he saw the telltale black mask and striped tail.

"Never saw a raccoon before?" Juniper asked.

"No. But I do know what they look like."

"It's amazing that these animals are showing themselves to us, but I hope no bears come around."

"What? Bears? Can we go back to the house?" Luther pleaded.

"I don't know what to do about Zorba. I don't have a horse trailer. I hate to leave him to fend for himself if the fire gets here."

"I don't think you have any choice, Juniper."

"Maybe I'll take him back to the pond so he can stay in the water if necessary."

"Doesn't he know to do that? Like the deer?"

"I'm just afraid he's disoriented with all this." She started coughing. "This smoke is getting worse."

"Please Juniper. Let's go. I know you love your horse and all, but they're waiting for us at the house and people do have to take priority."

She sighed. "Okay. I guess I have to trust his instincts."

Luther swished the flashlight beam all around them as they walked, while Juniper kept her flashlight pointed toward the ground. She wanted to make sure they didn't trip. "Do you think we should leave?" he asked.

"I don't really know what to do. We need to ask Dutch."

"You sure look like you know, all authoritative and no-nonsense."

"Well, it's an act. I'm just as scared as you are."

Luther took her hand again and they walked silently back toward the house. The problem was, they weren't sure where the house was. The lights were not on and they both started turning their flashlights in all directions. Finally they saw a chimney. "Why would they have turned off the lights?" Luther asked.

"The power probably went out."

"There goes our news source."

"We'll have to rely on our phones until the batteries go dead."

"Maybe it's time to leave," Luther said tentatively. "Better than taking any chances at staying."

"I don't know where to go with the load in the pick-up," Juniper replied.

"We'll just go to a motel or something. I'll stay in the truck to guard it."

"I'm sure all the motels are full." They reached the house and stumbled through the dark house to the living room. "Everyone okay?" Juniper called out as she shone the flashlight around the room.

"You finally got back!" Buster shouted. "Let's get the hell out of here!"

"Please can we go?" Scarlett begged.

"I think we should, Juniper," Tasha affirmed. "The last thing we heard before the television went out was that the fire was spreading south."

"Where's Dutch?" Juniper asked.

"He went out," Leo answered. "He said he had some other stuff to get. I don't know. He didn't really say where he was going."

"Let me call him. Hold on." She took out her phone. "Oh shit. I'm out of juice."

"Here!" Tasha and Luther said in unison as they both reached their phones out to her.

Juniper took Luther's. "Turn yours off Tasha so we'll have one with enough battery in case Luther's dies too."

"Dutch's number is in there," Luther said.

Juniper pressed the contact and waited. "He doesn't answer."

"Let's just go." Tasha was getting adamant. "There might not be time if we wait any longer."

"Better safe than sorry," Homer piped up.

Juniper exhaled loudly. "Okay. Scarlett you and the animals go with Tasha. Homer, you come with me. Buster, will you go with Luther in the truck?"

"My car is pretty full already too," Leo added. "Do you want me to see if I can find Dutch?"

"Would you mind?" Juniper asked. "I want to get Homer out of here. I'm afraid his lungs can't take it."

"Should we plan on a meeting place that I can tell Dutch?" Leo asked.

"Let's just stay in touch by phone. Ask Dutch to let us know where we should go when you find him."

They all scurried out, Scarlett carrying Minnie and with Gypsy at her heels. They got in their respective vehicles and the caravan was on its way.

18

LUTHER SHOT THROUGH THE SMOKY DARKNESS, HIS NERVES CAUSING HIM TO GRIND GEARS AND CLATTER ONTO THE ROCKY SHOULDERS AS HE TRIED TO NAVIGATE THE UNFAMILIAR ROADS. "Where'd you get your license — a Cracker Jack box?" Buster joked. "Maybe I should drive even though I don't think I've put my hands on a steering wheel for fifteen years."

"Well, it's been twenty for me and neither one of us has a license."

"I guess you wouldn't have one — ha!"

"Where do you think we're headed?"

"Beats me," Buster shrugged. "I don't know where the hell we are, no less where we're going. Just hope we don't lose Juniper in this exodus."

"You aren't the only one," Luther muttered, gritting his teeth and stepping on the gas to catch up with the dim taillights ahead.

Meanwhile, in the car Tasha was driving, Scarlett had a hard time keeping Minnie from freaking out. "I don't think Minnie has ever been in a car," Scarlett said.

"Well I wish she'd realize it's for her own good. I just hope Gypsy doesn't go after her."

"I think Gypsy is more scared of her than she is of Gypsy."

"That doesn't make a fight any less likely."

Scarlett sighed. "Well, I'm doing the best I can to settle them down."

"I know, I know," Tasha replied. "I'm just freaking out a little myself."

"I wish we had some idea where we were going. What if we lose Juniper?"

"Well, I guess we just keep driving until we're out of danger."

Juniper's car was just as filled with fear and apprehension as the other two vehicles. Although Juniper, at least, knew the area, but she had Homer to deal with. "How you doing, Homer?"

"Not so great." His words were starting to slur again.

"As soon as we're in a safe place I can find some more pot for you."

"Hey, look at that!" Homer's trembling hand pointed out the window toward the moon.

"What?"

"You see those clouds covering the moon?"

"Yeah?"

"They're shifting."

"What do you mean?" Juniper asked.

"Watch them."

"Just tell me what they're doing!"

"It looks like the wind might be coming from the southeast now."

"So the fire will be moving northwest?"

"Right."

"Are you sure?"

"Yeah I'm sure," Homer answered. Juniper put her right turn signal on. She pulled over, and fortunately Tasha and Luther followed suit. "Are we going to turn around?" Homer asked as Juniper got out of the car.

"No, but I just want to let them know what you said. I also need to use Tasha or Luther's phone to call Dutch and see if we can get more information."

"What's going on?" Luther shouted as he and Tasha came running up.

"Homer says the wind is shifting and the fire might be moving north now away from us," Juniper replied.

"How does he know?" Tasha asked.

"Look at the clouds in front of the moon. You can see how they're moving that way."

"So can we go back to the farm?" Luther wondered.

"Let me have your phone."

Luther handed Juniper his phone and went back to the truck to tell Buster the news while Tasha did the same for Scarlett. "Oh good. I'll take Gypsy out for a minute so she can pee." Gypsy bounded out and immediately started barking like crazy. "What is it Gypsy?"

"Heavens to Murgatroyd!" Buster yelled from the truck.

"Is that like Heavens to Betsy?" Tasha murmured to Scarlett.

"Different sex, I think," Scarlett snickered.

"What is it, Buster?" Luther called back.

"There's a fucking bear!" Buster answered.

The group turned around and Juniper shone her flashlight in the direction Buster pointed. She didn't need to, though. The truck's headlights revealed the large form of a bear. When Juniper aimed her light into its eyes, they reflected green. She wasn't sure what that meant, but they all scrambled back into their respective vehicles. "I can't find Minnie!" Scarlett cried. "She must have run out when I let Gypsy out!"

Scarlett opened the door and started to get out. "Scarlett!" screamed Tasha. "You can't go out there!"

"I've got to find Minnie!" Scarlett cried as she scurried away. Gypsy remained in the car, howling, as Tasha froze in fear at the scene that was unfolding.

"What the hell is Scarlett doing?" Luther exclaimed.

"Stupid girl!" barked Buster.

Homer pulled on Juniper's arm. "Why is Scarlett wandering around?"

Juniper cocked her head away from Luther's cell phone. "What do you mean?" Juniper followed Homer's finger, pointing at a frantic figure running back and forth to the road's shoulders. She put her window down and heard Scarlett yelling for Minnie. "Oh Jesus! She's looking for that cat!" Juniper opened her door and stood next to the car. "Scarlett! Get back in the car. You don't screw around with a bear!"

"I've got to find Minnie!" Scarlett cried, stumbling against the brush along the road.

Luther saw Juniper standing by her car and leapt into action. He was not about to let Juniper risk her life for Scarlett. Paying no attention to Buster's admonishments, he got out and ran toward Scarlett. "Get in the car!" he yelled at her.

"I see her! She's up that tree!" Scarlett screamed.

"I'll get her! You go back!" Luther grabbed her and shoved her back towards the cars. He could see Minnie up the tree, and also saw the bear starting to move toward him. He rushed to the tree and scrambled up it, surprising himself that he could climb a tree at all. He reached Minnie and grabbed her by her scruff until her claws gave way from the tree. Down below, the bear's glowing green eyes looked back up at him.

Juniper stuck her head through the car's open window. "Homer, should we make noise? Will that scare the bear away or make it worse?"

"Just be quiet. Luther's doing the right thing being still and calm. The bear is as scared as we are. Bears eat plants, not people."

Juniper got back in the car and kissed his cheek. "Thank you, Daniel Boone."

They watched as the bear studied Luther up in the tree for what seemed like a minute, and then turned away and scampered off. "All clear," Homer sighed.

Juniper ran out of the car toward the tree. "Are you alright?"

"Yeah, just take Minnie, will you?" Luther answered as he moved slowly down the tree and handed the cat off to Juniper.

Scarlett showed up at Juniper's side and took Minnie, "Oh baby, it's okay." Scarlett cooed as she took Minnie back to her car.

Juniper threw her arms around Luther when he got on solid ground and kissed him. "Watch out," Luther whispered as their lips parted. "People are watching!"

"Don't care," she breathed back. "Everyone stares at heroes."

Luther laughed. "I didn't even know I had it in me to climb a tree."

"You're full of surprises," she winked.

"So what did you find out? Can we go back to the farm?" he asked.

Juniper shook her head. "I haven't been able to reach any place that might help us. I don't think we should take a chance. Let's just drive south for now. I'll let Dutch know we are still driving south." They parted and the caravan was back on the road.

Meanwhile Leo had not found Dutch yet. He realized how stupid it was that he had been the one to offer to look for him. He didn't know the farm at all and didn't have any idea where to even look. He was coughing and his eyes were stinging. His asthma was really bad. He wanted to call Juniper and get some advice on where to look for Dutch, but he didn't have her number. He tried Luther's and Tasha's but neither answered. He wandered around for another fifteen minutes or so and then decided to go back to the house to wait there for Dutch. As he approached the house, he saw Dutch standing by Leo's car. "Where the hell have you been?" Dutch asked.

"Looking for you."

"Well, that was stupid. You wouldn't have known where to look."

"I figured that out only after I offered."

"Let's go. Just follow me. I'll try to call Juniper and see where they are, but we had better get out now."

They got into their cars and drove off. Just as they approached the gate Dutch stopped his car abruptly and got out. "I forgot something!"

"You're gonna go back?" Leo yelled at him. "Is it really that important?"

Dutch didn't answer and got back in his car and turned it around. Leo stood by his car, unsure what to do. Should he follow him or wait? He also realized that he hadn't gotten Dutch's number and Dutch didn't have his. He got back in the car to catch his breath. He hadn't kept important things handy, and he had just decided to quit a job he enjoyed to live on a farm in the middle of nowhere. Unless this fire kept moving towards it and burned it to the ground. Then what?

Dutch finally drove down to Leo's car and stopped. He got out and rapped on Leo's window. Leo put the window down. "Go on ahead. They're at a rest stop in Laytonville, about an hour south of here."

"What about you?"

"I still have stuff to do here."

"It's awfully dangerous. I think you should leave."

Dutch glared at Leo. "I'll make my own decisions . . . thanks."

Leo exhaled and shrugged. "Okay, fine." Dutch left him and got back in his car. Leo drove out the gate toward town and US 101, remembering Laytonville when he and Tasha made the trip to the farm. But as he drove, he had a nagging feeling that he shouldn't leave Dutch. And dammit! He still hadn't gotten his number. Maybe he should go to Garberville and see what was happening in town. At least he'd be near the freeway so he could leave quickly if he had to. Besides which, he was exhausted and didn't relish the thought of driving another hour and a half. Maybe he should just pull over someplace, find his inhaler, and sleep a little in the car. He did pull over, but just to try and figure out what to do. He felt bad leaving Dutch alone, even though that was clearly what Dutch wanted. He didn't see any point in driving to Laytonville and then most likely have to turn right around and come back. Driving to Garberville was probably the best option. Maybe the smoke wasn't as bad there.

He pulled into the downtown Shell gas station, the only place open all night in Garberville. He tried Tasha's and Luther's phones to see if they had heard from Dutch, but no answer. He had the hopeful thought that they were sleeping somewhere safe and had turned off their phones to save power. He was going to ask the clerk if he could park there and sleep a couple of hours, but realized that the sleepy clerk couldn't care less. He finally found his inhaler and used it, but it didn't seem to help much. He reclined his seat and closed his eyes, but as tired as he was, he was too wired to fall asleep. He pulled his seat up and started the engine. He would go to the Laytonville rest stop after all. The sun was starting to rise and he wanted to be with Tasha.

19

THE FARM CARAVAN JOINED A CROWD OF FIRE REFUGEES AT THE LAYTONVILLE REST STOP. Despite the late hour, cars were still jockeying for parking and there was a constant murmur of voices sharing their escape stories. Although they weren't exactly comfortable trying to stretch out in their vehicles, sleep soon overtook them all. When the sun rose a few hours later and woke them up, the stiffness of their joints was universal. "Homer, let me get Luther to help you to the bathroom," Juniper said as she opened her door and piled out, doing lunges as she walked to the truck to loosen up her legs.

"You look pretty funny," Luther said as he got out of the truck to greet her.

"It helps," she answered. "Could you take Homer to the restroom?"

"Sure." Luther put his head inside the truck. "Hey Buster. Homer and I are going to the restroom. Do you want to come?"

"What the hell – is this a pissing party?"

"Just asking. Don't have to be a grouch."

Buster laughed. "Well, at my age I better accept any invitation I get." He crawled out of the truck and tried to straighten up. "Homer okay?" he asked.

"He's doing remarkably well," Juniper answered.

Buster nodded and hobbled off with Luther to get Homer. Juniper walked to Tasha's car and found both she and Scarlett still asleep. Gypsy and Minnie were zonked out in the back seat, side by side. Juniper left them all alone and took Luther's phone out. She tried to call Cal Fire but couldn't get through and tried to think of who else she could call to get up to date information. "Damn! I just don't know the area north of us that well," she muttered.

Luther and Buster found Homer struggling to get out of the car. His hands and legs trembled and he had a hard time standing. He leaned on Luther as he helped him walk to the men's room, but it was slow going and Buster decided he couldn't wait. "I'm going on ahead. I'll warm the seat for you!" he cackled as he strode off.

"Good work with that black bear." Homer's speech hadn't deteriorated much and Luther took that to be a good sign. Maybe

Homer's walking difficulties and his shaking was more due to sleeping in an awkward position.

"I don't know how I climbed that tree. It's been a lot of years since I did that, if I ever did. We didn't have a lot of trees where I grew up."

"Hah! It's just instinct. Most of dealing with nature and animals is instinct. Lucky it wasn't a mama with a bunch of cubs around or you might not be here now walking an old man to take a dump."

"What do you mean?" Luther asked, starting to feel a bit alarmed.

"Black bears can climb trees, you know."

"But the bear was brown."

"Black bears aren't only black. They can be brown too."

"But how do you know it was a black bear?"

Homer laughed. "Hasn't been a grizzly in California for a hundred years."

"You got me all confused. Now you're talking about a grizzly bear?"

"You city boys!" Homer scoffed. "Brown bear and grizzly are the same. All bears here nowadays are black bears and they can be different shades. Grizzlies can't climb trees too well because of their rounded claws, but black bears can and will if provoked. You did the right thing being calm and quiet." Homer laughed.

"Maybe you just didn't smell like you tasted too good!"

"Jeez. Thanks a lot, Homer." Luther smiled and winked. They got to the restroom and joined Buster who was washing his face at the sink. "Can you make it to the stall?" Luther asked.

"I'll do it if it kills me. I ain't having you come in with me, that's for damn sure." Homer held onto the walls and eased into the stall.

When the trio left the restroom they ran into Scarlett and Tasha entering the ladies side. Gypsy was with them and Minnie was using a pile of leaves as a litter box. Juniper was leaning against the car, talking animatedly on the phone. She held out a vape pipe to Homer when the group arrived at her side. Homer took it and immediately put it in his mouth, nodding a thank you as he walked to a picnic table. Juniper handed Luther's phone back to him. "It needs charging."

"Where are Dutch and Leo?" Tasha asked as she approached.

"I'm not sure. I left a message that we were in Laytonville and would find a restaurant to eat and charge our phones."

"Why aren't they here then? You'd think they would have gotten here by now," Tasha said.

"I don't know Tasha," Juniper answered with irritation. "I haven't talked to Dutch."

"Aren't you worried?"

"Let's find that restaurant," Luther said, trying to soothe the frayed nerves. The procession began with Juniper and Homer in the lead. They stopped at Friends Coffee House and were pleased to find a café that lived up to its name. They parked themselves along with some like-minded travelers to relax a little, charge their phones, eat some breakfast, and ponder their next move.

After a couple of hours, the phones were charged, their stomachs were full, and the café was filling up with the lunch crowd. Homer and Buster had fallen asleep in the back seats of the cars and Scarlett had found a rope to use as a leash for Gypsy and was walking her around the town, what little there was of it. Minnie had found the bench out in front of the café a good place to curl up for a nap. Tasha, Luther and Juniper sat together and discussed their predicament. "I can't reach Dutch. I wonder if the cell towers are out. I think we should go back," Juniper said.

"Do you think he and Leo got separated somehow?" Tasha asked. "At least Dutch knows his way around the area."

"And what about Homer and Buster?" Luther asked. "They can't keep running from fire like we can."

"I know. But I feel terrible just leaving Dutch. And I'm worried about Zorba."

"Let's go back," Tasha piped in. "We'll fight the damn fire ourselves if we have to!" Tasha exclaimed.

"What? With a garden hose?" Luther snorted.

"Oh, I don't know. We'll figure it out."

"Homer will know," Juniper cut in. "He knows just about everything."

The three gathered their things and left the café. Scarlett was across the street and Tasha called out to her, "C'mon. We're going back."

"You have Minnie?" Scarlett asked.

"Oh, sorry. Forgot about her." Tasha scooped up the cat. "C'mon Minnie the Moocher!"

They got back into their respective vehicles and the convoy was underway for the trip back to the farm. Homer took a few tokes and fumbled with his ear buds. Juniper watched him work at them with no success. She considered stopping the car to help him, but then said, "Let's turn the radio on instead. It'll help pass the time for me."

"Sure, sweet pea," Homer said as he dropped the ear buds and reached for the radio button.

Juniper debated whether to let him struggle or do it for him and then decided to just ask. "Would you like me to do it?"

"It would probably be a lot faster." She turned on some music and watched how Homer's trembling body turned into one that swayed with the music.

Luther followed behind in the truck, relaxed and proud of his driving. Buster tried to play his guitar, but there wasn't enough room in the cab. "I should buy myself a ukulele for situations like this," Buster said.

Luther laughed. "You think you'll ever be in a situation like this again?"

"One never knows, does one?" Buster started singing.

'You just made that up?" Luther asked when Buster finished singing.

Buster shook his head. "I think I just heard your momma roll over in her grave. Billie Holiday. You got a lot of learnin' to do."

"Yes," Luther sighed. "I do."

Scarlett and Tasha also used music to pass the time by singing at the top of their lungs. They laughed and sang and Gypsy even chimed in with a howl every now and then. Minnie, in typical cat fashion, yawned and found the whole scene ridiculous. "We're very lucky," Scarlett said.

"Lucky?" Tasha looked at her curiously.

"To be able to get out of the awful situations we were in and find refuge."

"I'd rather not have my refuge threatened by fire," Tasha sighed.

"I'd rather be confronted with the consequences of nature than of people. This is the closest thing to a vacation I've ever had. The farm is kinda like a resort to me."

"Yes," Tasha smiled. "I guess it is kind of a last resort."

When they arrived in Garberville Juniper pulled into the deserted parking lot of Ray's Food Place. "They should know what's happening and I need to buy a few things," she told Homer. "Do you want to stay here or come inside?"

"I'll come." Homer got out of the car fairly easily and followed Juniper to the truck. Tasha and Scarlett soon joined the huddle.

"I'm picking up some stuff and I think they'll have a good idea where the fire's headed." She shot Homer and Buster a playful look. "Here's your chance to get some junk food."

Buster grabbed Homer's arm. "Let's go, Homer!"

The entourage entered the store and found the shelves somewhat bare and the lone cashier standing at her cash register scrolling through her phone. There were no other customers. Juniper approached the cashier. "Do you have any recent updates on the Bull Creek fire?"

The cashier shrugged. "Not really."

"Has Cal-Fire issued a mandatory evacuation?"

"I don't think it's mandatory, still just voluntary. I don't know if people have left town or they're just holed up in their houses."

"Okay, thanks. Hey, do you know if the cell towers are out?"

"That's what I heard."

Juniper told Tasha and Luther what the cashier had said. "At least our phones are charged if the power's still off when we get back to the farm and we'll be able to use them once they get the cell towers up and running again."

They split up and went through the aisles picking up food that wouldn't require refrigeration or cooking. "We should gas up before we go back too," Luther said as they stood at the cash register.

Tasha was the only one who tried to pay for any of it, but Juniper wouldn't let her. "You can pay for gas instead." Juniper then turned to Luther and handed him forty dollars. "Here's for gas for the truck." Luther took it sheepishly, but he really had no other choice. "There's a Shell station down the street."

"Yeah, I know it well. I spent my first night in Garberville hanging out inside its minimart."

They gathered the rest of the group and drove down to the gas station. It was open, but also deserted. Tasha got out to pump some gas. "The air is so bad!" Scarlett said.

"Stay in the car." Tasha joined Juniper and Luther at the pumps.

"I wonder if the True Value is open," Juniper said. "We should get some respiratory masks. Dutch has some paint masks, but they won't do."

"What's the difference?" Luther asked.

"Big difference. Dust or surgical masks don't filter out smoke particles. Maybe I should go get masks and the rest of you go back to the farm. I'll meet you there."

"No," Tasha added. "Homer needs to get back sooner. Why don't Scarlett and I go? That makes more sense."

"But you don't know where it is," Juniper countered. "And then you have to know how to get back to the farm from Redway."

"Hey, Juniper. I'm a big girl," Tasha snapped back. "I've been around. I can find the store and the return route to the farm."

"I didn't mean you're incompetent," Juniper retorted.

"Ladies. Please." Luther sighed. "We are all tired and cranky, but Tasha's right about Homer. Plus it makes more sense for Juniper to be at the farm since she knows where everything is." Juniper glared at Luther and he wished he hadn't used the term *ladies* but he was exhausted and too irritable to apologize. "Just tell Tasha where the store is and what she needs to get," he said as he put his arm around Juniper. She squirmed out of the crook of his arm and walked away.

Tasha rolled her eyes at him. "I'll find it." She started walking back to her car. "At least I know it's in Redway!"

Luther finished putting gas in the truck and went inside to pay. "Do you know what direction the fire's going?" Luther asked.

"Nah. The last people here said it keeps changing."

"At least you have power," Luther answered.

"For now. It was off last night but came back on this morning."

"Do you know if cell towers are out?"

"I don't know. I think cell service has been going in and out."

Luther hoped that was also the case at the farm. He looked out the window and saw

Tasha drive off and Juniper idling in her car, waiting for him to follow. "Thanks," he said when the clerk gave him his change. He nodded at Juniper before getting in the truck but she ignored him. He pulled up behind her and she took off.

"What's with those two?" Buster asked.

"Tasha's going to a hardware store to get us some masks."

"So why is Juniper wound tighter than a clock?"

Luther laughed. "You know? I'm not really sure."

"Women," Buster said as he shook his head. "Can't live with 'em, can't live without 'em."

"Not sure I agree," Luther replied. "I lived without them for too long."

20

THE FARM LOOKED EERIE THROUGH AN AMBER PALL OF SMOKE. Juniper got out and put in the code to open the gate. The car and truck moved slowly up the driveway, everyone checking out the environs to see if there had been any fire damage. "Looks like we haven't been touched yet," Homer said.

"Yeah, everything looks intact," Juniper answered, breathing a sigh of relief. "As soon as we get inside and you're comfortable, I need to go out and look for Zorba."

'Sure, honey," Homer said, patting her knee. "I'll be fine with Luther and Buster hovering over me just like Jewish mothers. Damn! They never leave me alone for a second." Juniper smiled when Luther and Buster were at his door as soon as they stopped. "See what I mean?" Homer said.

Buster opened the door. "C'mon Homer. Let's get out of this breath from Hades. I need to sleep. I feel like I been rode hard and hung up to dry." Homer laughed and climbed out of the car. He teetered and Luther and Buster both grabbed him and they walked arm in arm in arm to the house.

Juniper brought the groceries into the kitchen and dumped the bags on the counter. She tied a scarf around her nose and mouth, knowing full well that it probably wouldn't do her lungs any good. But maybe it would make it a little easier to breathe. Then she went out to look for Zorba. She checked the pasture where he usually hung out, but it was empty. She went to his shed and saw that he had at least eaten the food she had left. Or some animal did. She saw some deer running amok, unable to figure out where to go to escape the smoke. The scene was not the usual peaceful picture of deer grazing, frogs croaking and birds chirping. It was eerily quiet. Luther came running up to her. "I thought I'd find you here," he said as he leaned against a tree, gasping for breath.

"It's probably not a good idea to run in this hazardous air," Juniper said curtly.

"Give me a break, will you?" Luther countered with a mix of irritation and desperation. "We're all tired and anxious. I'm sorry if I offended you."

Juniper studied him for a minute and then managed a little smile. She gave him a peck on the lips. "Do you want to help me look for Zorba?"

"I don't know if that's the wisest thing to do right now. Homer thinks we should get prepared to fight the fire if it gets close."

Juniper paused for a minute. "He's probably right. Did he say how?"

Luther shrugged. "I think we could at least locate hoses and buckets or something. Let's go ask Homer." He took her hand and they walked back to the house.

"I didn't even check if the power is on," Juniper sighed.

"I forgot, too. I could see what I was doing without turning on the lights."

They got to the kitchen and tried the switch. No lights. "Shit!" Juniper said as she opened the refrigerator. "The fruit and vegetables might be okay. Just the dairy stuff would go bad this fast." She quickly took out some fruit and got some plates. "Would you carry the bags? Let's eat while we strategize." They took the food into the living room and found both Buster and Homer snoring on the sofas.

"Maybe we should wait to eat," Luther whispered.

"I guess so."

They heard the kitchen door open and Tasha, Scarlett, and the animals scurried in. "We got the masks!" Scarlett gushed as she opened a bag and threw the masks on the coffee table. "The guy at the hardware store said the wind had shifted again and was coming from the north. That's bad for us, right?"

Juniper nodded and turned to Homer. She gently shook his shoulder. "Homer?" Homer opened his eyes. "The fire's coming towards us now. What do you suggest we do?"

Homer took a couple of deep breaths and sat up. "We need to hose down the roof, clean the gutters, and fill all the tubs and basins with water. Block any vents you see."

"With what?" Luther asked.

"I don't know. Wood? Just nail something over it. Whatever you can find. Find a hoe, a pick, a shovel . . . a hatchet and pole saw would be better." He turned to Juniper. "Is there a chainsaw?"

"I think so."

"What are we supposed to do with all these tools?" Tasha asked.

"Start clearing the brush and small trees on the north side of the house."

"Which way is north?" Luther asked.

"The opposite of south," Buster added.

"What direction from the house?!" Luther demanded.

"Don't get your knickers all tied up in a knot! I was just kidding."

Juniper tapped Luther on the shoulder and pointed. "That's north."

"Homer and I will stay inside and fill up the tubs and basins. How many bathrooms Dutch got?" Buster asked.

Juniper counted silently. "I think four. There's a tub in the laundry room too. And of course the sink in the kitchen."

"I'll find 'em. You young people go out and cut down the trees and brush." Buster looked at Juniper. "Where's the hose? I can do the roof when I'm done."

"You think you can do that, Buster?" Luther asked.

"Don't put me out to pasture just yet!"

Luther reached out to Buster. "Seems I'm offending everyone today."

Buster shrugged him off. "Let's just get to work." He then tuned to help Homer up. "C'mon old man. We got work to do. Hold it. I just remembered. You can't hose down the roof if there's no power, let alone fill a bathtub. You need the pump working to do that."

"There's a little portable gasoline pump we use to move water between irrigation tanks," Juniper offered. "It should give enough pressure to throw water on the roof if you put a small nozzle on the hose. If we can get it started, that is."

"I'll go outside and find hoses to put through the windows," Buster said. "Homer can fill the tubs."

"And if the hoses are long enough to reach the house," Luther muttered as Scarlett handed out masks.

"Where are the tools?" Tasha asked.

"Follow me." Juniper led the group to an outbuilding. She pointed to a bunch of tools leaning against a wall inside. "I have to look for the chain saw. I'm not sure where Dutch keeps that."

"Did you call him?" Luther asked. "Does he know we're back on the farm?"

Juniper shook her head and ran out. Luther picked up lopping shears. "What about these?" he asked Tasha.

She took the shears. "Yeah. These are good. Let's take as much as we can carry and see what works."

Luther picked up a hatchet and a spade. Scarlett took a shovel and a hoe. Tasha carried two pruning shears, one long-handled and one small one. The three left the building. "So which way is north from here?" he asked.

"Shit. I don't know." Tasha looked over at the house. "Let me think. Juniper was standing this way when she pointed."

Just then Juniper showed up lugging a chain saw. "I've got to find some gas for this."

"Do you want help?" Luther asked.

"No. I'm okay."

"Hey Juniper. Is north that way?" Tasha asked.

Juniper shook her head and grinned. "You guys are hopeless. No, over there." She pointed and ran off in her continued search for gasoline while the other three took off toward the north side of the farm.

They got to a brushy area and Tasha immediately got to work. Scarlett and Luther looked at each other ruefully. "We are kinda hopeless," Luther whispered to Scarlett as they watched Tasha confidently attack the brush.

"Maybe we're overthinking this," Scarlett replied.

"Uh huh. Maybe we just need to use our instincts." Luther took the axe and started whacking.

Scarlett looked at the shovel and hoe she was carrying. "I wonder why Homer said to get these."

"They're just tools to use for cutting and tamping down the brush and putting out fires," Tasha replied.

"Okay," Scarlett answered. She turned to Luther. "I think she has more instinct than we do."

"Just work on that dry grassy patch with the hoe," Tasha grunted as she lopped off a thick branch.

Juniper joined them in a few minutes and dropped the chainsaw. "Anyone know how to start this thing?" she asked.

Luther looked at Tasha. She shrugged and shook her head. "Maybe we need to get Homer or Buster," he said walking over to Juniper and turning the chainsaw over in his hands.

"We ought to be able to figure it out," she replied.

"I don't know. Looks pretty dangerous if you don't know what you're doing. I'll go ask Homer to show me." Luther took the chainsaw and handed Juniper the hatchet. "You can take over for me."

When Luther got back to the house he found Buster outside fumbling with the hose. "Homer's finishing filling those tubs with water. Thought I'd go ahead and work on the roof, but man, you can't breathe out here!" Buster said.

"Where's your mask?" Luther asked.

"Aaah, I don't like that thing."

"But that's what it's for!"

"Awright, you go in and get me that mask. Homer's probably done by now."

Luther went inside and found Homer in the kitchen. "Hey Homer!" Luther called to him, but Homer had his ear buds in and was dancing around unable to hear him. Luther tapped him on the shoulder.

"Oh, hey there, Luther. You couldn't have finished chopping up that brush already."

"I came in to get Buster a mask. We need help starting that chainsaw."

"I'll go with you."

"You shouldn't be out in that smoke, Homer."

"Neither should you. I'll be okay. Long as I keep the music going."

Luther shrugged. "Okay, but you'll need to wear a mask too." Luther ran into the living room and scooped up the two masks laying on the coffee table.

The three men gathered in front of the house where Buster was aiming the hose at the roof. Homer and Buster put on their masks and Luther took Homer's arm to steady him.

"Have you used a chainsaw before?" asked Homer.

"No."

"Well, a couple of things — most important, whenever you cut don't let the saw drop towards your leg. You'll find a chainsaw doesn't cut, it shreds. Just a touch of the moving chain to any part of your body will do more damage than you can imagine."

"That's reassuring," frowned Luther.

"Starting it can be difficult, especially when the saw is cold. First, pull out that little handle on the back of the carburetor."

"Huh?"

Homer chuckled. "Okay, that red thing on the back of the saw. You'll push it back in a few — maybe ten seconds after the saw starts. Then push down on that little black button on the top of the saw — right there," Homer pointed. "That temporarily eliminates the cylinder compression making it easier to pull. Okay, now put your foot on the handle and yank the cord upward."

Luther pulled. "Nothing's happening."

"I said yank it! Push in the decompression button again and yank it like you mean it."

Luther tried a few more times and the saw finally started. "Look at that!"

"Quick! Push in the choke before it dies!" Homer shouted over the din.

Gypsy ran around barking at the noisy chainsaw while Minnie settled on a tree branch for a snooze, seemingly unbothered by the noise or the smoke. Juniper went back to chopping with the hatchet while Luther looked around and then started sawing.

The three women and Luther continued working as Homer went around giving advice until it got too dark to work. "I've got to get back to the house and gather the flashlights and candles," Juniper called out.

"Thank God!" Scarlett gasped. I'm exhausted!"

The group trekked back to the house and collapsed in the living room. Buster was already sleeping on a sofa. It wasn't long before the whole group, including the animals, was fast asleep.

21

LEO HAD ARRIVED AT THE REST STOP IN LAYTONVILLE THAT MORNING, BUT NO ONE FROM THE FARM WAS THERE. He tried calling Tasha and Luther, but neither answered. He considered whether he should wait for Dutch. He hadn't a clue what to do. He thought about continuing to drive south and going to his apartment in Sacramento to wait it out, but he wanted to be with Tasha. There was no doubt now that he had fallen for her hard. But he didn't know whether she was back at the farm. They could be anywhere if the fire had closed in. And being at the farm would be a terrible decision for him with his asthma.

He checked the map on his phone and saw it was about a three-hour drive to Sacramento. He would need to go back at some point anyway to pack and get things in order. He also needed to meet with the union leaders. That definitely seemed like the wisest move. He dialed Tasha. "I'm going to my apartment to get a few things. Please call and tell me where you are." He drove off resolved that this was, in fact, the best decision. He got to his apartment about noon and had just gotten out of the shower when his phone rang. "Tasha?" he answered eagerly.

"No, not Tasha."

"Oh, hey Gordon."

"I heard about the fire. Is it near you?"

"Pretty close. But I'm actually back in Sacramento. We had to evacuate, but more importantly, I've decided to leave the union."

"What?!"

"Dutch asked me to stay on the farm and help him organize a music festival."

"Huh? What the hell do you know about music festivals?"

"Organizing is organizing. I can figure it out. And I need to do something else. Dutch is cool, the farm is nice and you were right, Tasha and I are getting closer and closer. I want to be with her."

"Jesus, Leo. What have you been smoking?"

"I thought about it a lot. I'm ready. I think this music festival thing could really hit it big and then we could make it a yearly thing."

"Just don't burn any bridges. You have no idea how this will all turn out."

"Thanks Mama Gordon!"

"Damn right," he replied. "Now tell me, how's Luther doing?"

"Really well. Have you talked to him?"

"Not really. Ask him to call me, will you? I didn't want to bring him back into the lawsuit until he'd had some time to acclimate to his new surroundings. But that's not why I was calling."

"What's up?" Leo asked.

"I got a phone call from a guy looking for you. He said he was with the union, but it sounded to me like he was fishing for information. Have you told the union that you're leaving?"

"Yeah, but I didn't elaborate. What did he say?"

"I don't really remember, but he knew enough about you and the union that I thought he was legit. I thought it was strange at first, but now I guess it has to do with your plans."

"I gotta go, Gordon. Thanks for letting me know. I'll be in touch." Leo hung up and hurriedly got dressed, packed some more things and called the union headquarters to tell them he'd be in shortly.

When he got outside his apartment and opened his car door, he noticed a van parked across the street with Oasis Florist, Las Vegas, painted on the side. Weird that they would they drive over five hundred miles to deliver flowers? He got in and drove off, glancing at his rear view mirror periodically. He half expected the strange van to follow him, but he never noticed it.

He spent most of the day meeting with the regional manager and a coworker who would temporarily take over his position. He thought he'd be driving back to Garberville that evening, but he was exhausted and decided to wait until the morning. He wanted to try Tasha again, but he was beginning to feel that there was more going on than just her phone being off. Why hadn't she called? He put it out of his mind and fell asleep.

The harsh ring of Juniper's phone woke up the troops. She fumbled to find it in the dark and looked at the screen. It was Dutch! "Hello?" she answered.

"Sorry to call so late. Are you at the farm?" Dutch asked.

"Yeah," she answered, sitting up and blinking through the gloom at Homer and Buster on the sofas. Nearby, Tasha and Scarlett were sprawled in chairs and Luther was lying next to her on the floor. "Where are you?"

"What's going on there?" he asked, ignoring her question.

"I don't know. It's smoky as hell and we cut down some trees and brush to the north."

"You did?" Dutch asked.

"Homer told us we needed to." Juniper saw that Luther's eyes were open, watching her. "It's Dutch," she mouthed to him.

"Good," Dutch replied. "Listen to Homer. He'll know what to do. Is everyone okay?"

"Yeah. How come you didn't answer earlier?" Juniper asked.

"Did Leo call Tasha?" Dutch countered. "He went to Laytonville, I think."

"Not that I know of, but we had the phones turned off most of the time to save juice. And then I think cell service has been spotty."

"Tell Tasha to call him and tell him he can come back."

"So you didn't go to Laytonville?"

"I'll see you in a little bit." He hung up.

Juniper turned to Luther and whispered, "That was weird. He didn't go to Laytonville, but he won't tell me where he is. He said he'd be back soon."

"Good," Luther sighed in relief. "It feels strange cutting down all his forest when he isn't even here."

"He wants Tasha to call Leo and tell him he should come back."

"Leo's not with him?"

"Apparently not. I guess I should wake up Tasha to call Leo. I don't have his number."

"Wait, I have it in my phone. I can call him." He turned on his phone and noticed that Leo had called him a couple of times. "Hey Leo, it's Luther. We all had our phones turned off to save our batteries. We're back at the farm. Dutch just called and said to call you to come back."

"Has the fire been contained?"

"Not yet, but the wind has shifted and we've been cutting a fire break near the house."

"It's still pretty smoky then? My asthma was really bad up there."

"Yeah, but Tasha bought us special masks to wear and it's okay inside the house."

Leo sighed. "Is Tasha with you?"

"She's sleeping. We're all in the living room so we can leave quickly if we need to. There's no power."

"Okay. Thanks for calling. I'll see you soon." They hung up.

Luther pulled Juniper into his arms and kissed her. "Do you want to go upstairs?" he murmured.

"I gotta say, Luther, that I am just too tired to move."

Luther nodded. "Okay. I understand." They kissed.

"Who called?" Tasha called out.

Juniper rolled her eyes at Luther. "Dutch. He and Leo will be back soon," she answered. She didn't want to go into the whole story.

Soon the others started stirring. "Damn!" Luther whispered to Juniper. "They're all waking up now."

"I need to use the bathroom," Homer said. "Who's got a flashlight?"

Luther found a flashlight and went to the sofa to help Homer who was shaking pretty badly. "Can you make it?" Luther asked. "Do you want to vape first?"

"Dammit!" Homer tried to raise himself but couldn't get control of the tremors well enough. "I guess I did too much."

Luther put his arms around Homer's chest and lifted him off the sofa. "Can you walk?" Luther asked.

"I don't know." Juniper approached with a filled vape pipe and Homer's iPod in her hands. Luther stuffed the buds into his ears and turned it on. "Bbb a-ttt -ery's dead."

"Okay," Juniper sighed. "Take a couple of tokes then."

Buster sat up and reached for his guitar and started playing some blues. Homer smiled at him and then took a couple of tokes. He took a couple of steps and Luther helped him to the bathroom. "Hit it, Buster," Homer said over his shoulder as he left.

Tasha stirred, got up and walked to the window. "Doesn't the glow from the fire look closer?"

Juniper came to her side. "That isn't a glow, that's the flicker of flames!" The two of them ran out the door with Scarlett and Gypsy right behind. "Oh man, there's a grass fire over there by the trimmers' barn! Tasha and Scarlett, grab the shovels!" Juniper ran around the back of the house dragging the hose with her. She turned on the gasoline water pump and held the hose toward the embers that were burning just a few feet from the barn, but the water didn't reach. "Use the shovels and beat down the embers!"

"It's not working!" Scarlett shouted as she hit at the fire.

Buster appeared and yelled," Turn the embers over while you're beating!"

Tasha and Scarlett did as they were told while Juniper filled a couple of buckets with water. Luther arrived just in time to carry the buckets to the fire and toss the water into the flames. A puff of steam went into the night sky, followed by the acrid smell of damp ashes. Luther stood, coughing and staring all around for the telltale glow of embers. "Shit!" Juniper exclaimed. "I didn't realize embers could fly so far!"

"Maybe we need to leave someone outside to keep watch," Luther said.

"I think so," Juniper agreed.

"I'll go first," Luther said. "Just gonna go inside and get my mask. He ran around to the front door and the others followed at a more leisurely pace.

"What's in that barn?" Tasha asked. You called it the trimmers' barn?"

"It's where the trimmers live during harvest," Juniper answered.

Luther met the rest of them at the front door. "Homer's not doing well at all. His breathing is really labored."

"He just needs to rest," Juniper said as she walked past him.

Luther went outside and found Gypsy wandering around, barking in various directions at nothing Luther could see through the smoky haze. "What are you barking at Gypsy?" he asked as he settled into an old Adirondack chair next to the barn. He had a shovel and a bucket of water on the ground beside him. His eyes were heavy and he had to work hard at keeping them open, but Gypsy's barking would not allow him to fall asleep.

He finally decided to walk around and see if he could figure out what was driving the dog crazy. He saw not one horse, but five, standing around in a pasture. Their eyes radiated fear and confusion. "Zorba?" he called out but felt foolish when he realized horses probably didn't come when called like dogs. They looked at him with such intensity. He felt instinctively that he should pet them and reassure them, but he was also a little afraid of them. He'd never been around horses before, and he was a stranger to them, even Zorba. He turned and ran back to the house to tell Juniper that Zorba had returned.

"Juniper!" he whispered as he entered the living room and shone the flashlight around the room. She wasn't on the floor where they had been laying earlier. The others were in their prior positions, but Juniper was nowhere to be found. Luther didn't know whether to look for her or go back to his sentry position. He decided to go back with a quick stop in the kitchen. She wasn't there so he went back outside and saw Juniper petting Zorba.

She looked up when Luther got close. "Hey," she smiled. "Look who's here."

Luther went up to the gleaming black horse, trusting that Juniper knew how to keep Zorba and his companions calm. He put his hand tentatively on Zorba's mane and stroked it. "Do you know these other horses?" he asked.

"No. They probably ran off from somewhere — or their owners let them loose in a desperate attempt to keep them safe."

"They're all scared."

"Yes. And Gypsy's constant barking isn't helping matters."

"Maybe I should bring her inside to Scarlett?" Luther asked.

"Except she might be good to have as a lookout. Not just for fire but also for other animals."

"You mean animals that might not be as tame as horses?" Luther asked with trepidation.

Juniper kissed him. "You are a funny man. Usually animals are much more afraid of you then you are of them."

"Did you come out here to check on me or look for Zorba?" he grinned.

"Both. But now that I'm here, I think I'll stay awhile."

"Don't you want to sleep?"

"Can't sleep. I think I'll take a ride around the farm and make sure all is well." She took hold of Zorba's halter and led him toward the trimmers' barn. "Could you hold him a minute while I get some rope to tie onto his halter?"

Luther put his hand out tentatively and took hold of the halter while Juniper went inside the barn. He decided that talking in a soothing voice to Zorba would calm his own nerves. "It's okay, boy," he cooed, mimicking every cowboy movie he ever saw. Zorba gazed back at him as if he were an idiot.

Juniper came back out, tied a couple of ropes to the halter to use as reins and somehow managed to swing herself onto Zorba's back. "I'll be back soon," she called out as she rode off. Luther settled back into the Adirondack chair and noted that the sun was beginning to come out surrounded by a red and yellow aura. The sky

looked orange and the smoke was so thick that
even the masks weren't helping. He started
second guessing their plan to stay on the farm,
but knew the decision wasn't his.

22

THE LIVING ROOM WAS FULL OF PEOPLE AND ANIMALS IN VARIOUS POSES OF FITFUL SLEEP. Tasha was the first to rise. She stretched and yawned and wandered aimlessly over to a bookshelf. Spying a *Sunset Western Garden Book*, she pulled it down and flipped through the pages. It was twenty years old, but that didn't really matter. She gazed out the window at the orange morning, and decided to finish reading while taking the next watch. "Might as well do something constructive while on sentry duty," she said to herself. She put on her mask and wandered outside and around the back of the house.

"Some lookout you are."

Luther opened his eyes. "Are you my relief?"

"Yep. Go inside and get some real sleep. But first get some of the others up and working on the brush that's too close to the house."

"How close is too close?" he asked.

"Homer says a hundred feet."

"Maybe we've already cleared that much."

"Maybe. It was so dark when we left, I couldn't tell."

Luther nodded and gazed around him, but the murky landscape showed no signs of fire nearby. He walked back to the house and found Homer and Buster gone from their customary couch positions, so he was able to lie on something relatively comfortable instead of the floor. He was almost asleep when he heard Tasha shouting and banging on one of the windows. Luther sat up and tried to figure out what she was saying. He couldn't make it out, but then he heard Juniper's voice. "Homer! Buster! Where are you? You need to get out!"

Luther scrambled off the couch and ran into Juniper who was running through the hall. "What's going on?" he asked.

"The fire! It's close to the house! Tasha saw some embers fly over the barn! We've gotta find Homer and Buster!"

"Have you tried their bedrooms or the bathroom?"

"I'll look. You go outside and help Tasha and Scarlett work on the fire!"

Luther ran outside and found Tasha and Scarlett pounding at little spot fires caused by falling embers. The larger fire was only about fifty feet from the house. Luther picked up two buckets and ran back to the hose. He started the portable pump and filled the buckets. He started to run back to the fire, causing the water to slosh out. "Dammit!" He turned his jogging into fast walking. He dumped the buckets of water onto a few of the little fires as the women swat at others with their shovels, and then he ran back to the hose to refill. Juniper ran up and grabbed two more buckets. "Did you find Homer and Buster?"

"They're coming," she answered breathlessly. "I told them to get in the car and truck to be ready to leave if necessary, but they refused."

The two men staggered over. "Is this the only fire?" Homer asked.

"As far as we know," Luther answered.

"Get another shovel and clear all the brush around it that might catch! Buster and I will help fill the buckets!"

Luther ran to find another shovel, but all he could find was a hoe. He got back just as another ember fell onto a small bush, igniting it. He hoed around the bush, trying to toss the dirt onto flames. Homer appeared holding a shovel with a short, broken handle. Luther stooped down with the tool, tossing dirt over the fire until it was just a smoking pile.

"Should I work on the perimeter?" Luther asked.

"Yeah. That's more important now."

They all worked at keeping the fire away from the house along the perimeter by turning dirt over the creeping flames. "It's almost like a flood!" gasped Juniper as she paused to wipe the sweat from her brow.

"I'd be alright with one of those right now!" Tasha replied.

Buster came up to them. "Homer says the wind's shifted away from the house. The fire should start tracking onto itself."

"Then what?" asked Scarlett.

"Well, uh, I guess it can't burn what's already burned."

"Sounds good," Scarlett sighed. "I'm exhausted."

"It doesn't help that we haven't exactly slept much these last couple of days," Tasha added.

Scarlett rested her chin on the end of her shovel handle and then gave a start. "Hey? Has anyone seen Gypsy and Minnie?"

Everyone looked at one another. "No," Juniper finally said.

"I've got to find them!" Scarlett let her shovel fall to the ground and ran off to search for them.

"I hope she doesn't trip over Homer," Buster muttered.

"Why would she do that?" Tasha asked.

"He's looking for a nice secluded place."

"For what?" Luther asked.

Buster rolled his eyes. "What do you think?"

"Oh. Is he okay by himself? Maybe he needs help."

"For God's sake, Luther," Buster chuckled. "Give the man some privacy will ya?"

A few minutes later, Scarlett came back with Minnie in her arms, Homer by her side, and Gypsy following close behind. "I found Gypsy and Minnie guarding Homer."

Homer laughed. "I told them I was fine, but they wouldn't leave."

"It didn't take them long to decide this is their home and they need to protect it and us," Tasha said.

"Yeah, it's a good thing we came back to the farm," Luther said. "We might have saved the house."

"Not might have," Homer answered. "We did."

They were all quiet for a minute. Finally Juniper spoke. "I think I'd better call Dutch and tell him." Luther watched her as she walked off, wondering if he should follow.

"Can we go find something to eat?" Scarlett sighed. "I'm starved and so are the animals."

"We need to really make sure there aren't embers burning underneath," Homer said.

"You mean keep turning the soil?" Tasha asked.

"Yep."

"Oh man!" Scarlett groaned.

Luther and Tasha immediately got to work and after a couple more minutes of moaning about it, Scarlett joined them. "Shall I get some more buckets of water?" Buster asked.

"No," Homer answered. "Find another tool of some kind. We all need to be turning the dirt."

They worked silently for several more minutes and Juniper arrived with a bag of water bottles and snacks. They all flopped on the ground and took their masks off to eat and drink.

Leo arrived in Garberville after an apprehensive trip. The van was outside his house when he left, but he didn't see it following him on the highway. He drove into the Ray's Food Place parking lot. Since the power might still be off at the house, he bought some perishables that they could all eat right away. He bought some fruit and vegetables, and some milk and cheese. While he was talking to the cashier about the latest fire news, Dutch appeared. "Have you been back to the farm yet?" he asked.

"Dutch! Where were you? I thought I'd meet you in Laytonville. I just got back here — thought I'd bring some food back to the farm."

"Yeah, my thought as well." He looked over the food lined up on the belt, waiting to be put into bags. "Did you bring any bags?"

"No."

"I'll give you some paper ones, no charge," the clerk piped in.

"Thanks," Leo smiled to the clerk. He turned back to Dutch. "You still haven't told me where you were. Did you stay at the farm?"

"I'll meet you there." Dutch replied as he turned away. He did, however, wait in the parking lot for Leo to get into his car and follow him. They arrived at the gate to the farm and Dutch got out to put in the code. He walked over to Leo's car and said, "We need to leave the gate open for now."

"To make it easier to escape?"

"And if fire engines need to come in."

"Jesus! It's really hard to breathe!" Leo coughed as his window rolled shut.

Gypsy had settled in as resident watchdog and barked incessantly at Dutch and Leo as they got out of their cars. "Hey, I'm the one who brings home the bacon. Better get used to me," Dutch said as he petted her.

The whole gang ran into the hallway to greet Dutch and Leo. Even Minnie decided to amble lazily over to see what all the excitement was. After hugs and excitedly talking of their day fighting off the fire, Leo said, "I bought some perishables."

Buster took the bags and asked, "Did you get anything good to eat?"

"Sorry, just healthy stuff. Where's Tasha?"

"She's still on sentry duty," Luther answered.

"And where's that?"

"In the back. I'll show you." Luther took Leo around the house.

"So the power's still out?" Dutch asked Juniper.

"Yes. We're using the portable water pump so we have water for the horses and to help fight the fire."

Dutch nodded. "You seem to have everything under control. Thanks. You've all done a great job here. I'm going to make some calls. How are you charging your phones?"

"We're not. We're just not using them unless we have to," Juniper said.

"Well, my car will charge them even when it's not running via the USB port, so we can all take turns charging if we need to. Any word from anyone on when the power might be back on?"

"We don't know, not using our phones and all. I guess I can call PG&E now." Juniper went in the house to find her phone and Dutch went back to his car. He returned to the house carrying an old beat up guitar case.

"Hey, Gypsy," Scarlett called as she put her mask back on. "Let's go for a walk." They walked around to the back of the house. Luther was sitting in the Adirondack chair. "Where's Tasha?" Scarlett asked.

"She wanted to show Leo where the fire had been."

Scarlett walked over to where the smoldering ashes had been and found Tasha kissing Leo. "C'mon Gypsy," Scarlett sighed and turned around to go in the other direction.

The wind had picked up and was thankfully blowing to the northeast, away from the farm. Juniper had finally reached someone at PG&E, and they told her they expected power to be restored by seven pm. Things were definitely looking up, and the atmosphere in the house turned more cheerful. Juniper had tried to prepare a mishmash of a dinner, based on what she could use that had survived the absence of refrigeration and didn't require cooking.

"Now what the hell are we eating?" Buster said as he sat down at the table.

"Just be happy there's anything to eat," Juniper replied.

They ate quietly, too tired to attempt conversation. Dutch broke the silence. "I want to thank all of you for saving the farm. It seems that the crisis is over so we can move forward with the music festival. We have a tentative date in May. Even though I'm not planting that much this year, I'd like to have the festival before we transplant the clones outside."

"What about fixing up the barn?" Luther asked.

"That's still going to happen. I want to get some animals and make this a real working farm, as self-sustaining as possible including the electricity so we don't have to live like this." Dutch finished by poking at the food before him.

"Do you want the animals here before the music festival?"

Dutch smiled at Luther. "Got to have something to keep you guys busy besides wildfires."

Just then there was a pounding on the door. "Sounds like the devil!" Buster exclaimed.

"I'll get it," Juniper said starting to get up. The pounding got louder.

"Hold on," Dutch said. "Luther, you and I go. And let me get my rifle."

The others looked uneasily at each other as Dutch and Luther left the candlelit kitchen.

Luther blinked in the darkness of the rest of the house. "I'll get the flashlight. It's in the living room."

They met at the front of the house, Luther shining the flashlight at the door and Dutch pointing his rifle at it. "Who is it?" Dutch asked.

"Just need some directions," a man answered. "We're lost."

Luther glanced at Dutch to see if he believed it. Dutch nodded at Luther to open the door while he kept his rifle aimed at it. Standing in front of them in the blinding glare of the flashlight were three men. One let out a low whistle. "Whoa, you don't need to be so unfriendly."

"We're looking for a guy named Leo. He here?" one of the other men said.

"You said you needed directions," Luther said icily.

"We do. Directions to Leo," the man chuckled.

"Get off my property," Dutch said.

"Just let us talk to Leo. We ain't gonna do anything to him. We just need to ask him some questions. We know he's here."

"Get off my property!"

"Look. We don't want any trouble. It's just business. Nothing's gonna happen to him."

At that moment Buster appeared out of the darkness. "I just rang up the sheriff," he said coolly.

"Hold on, old man. We don't mean no harm." The men glanced at each other and the one who had done most of the talking nodded toward the van. "Let's go. There are other ways to find her." The three men got in the van and drove off.

"So much for keeping the gate open," Dutch said. "Good thinking, Buster. Calling the sheriff."

"Especially when I don't have one of them cell phones," Buster snickered.

"Uh huh," Dutch replied, shaking his head. "And I heard the sheriff reply she'd be out here in forty-five minutes if we were lucky."

"What the hell are you two talking about?" Luther demanded.

"Would you go close the gate?" Dutch said as he gave Buster a sly smile.

Luther started to leave and stopped. "Wait a minute. Did he say there were other ways to find *her*?"

"He did," Dutch replied with a knowing look. "Maybe it isn't Leo they want."

Luther shrugged and walked down the driveway, careful to make sure the van was off the property before locking the gate. He turned to walk back to the house and noticed the van stopped down the road. A shiver passed through him and he trotted back to the house. When he got there, he found the group huddled around the table, listening to Dutch's account of the encounter with the three men.

"Are they gone?" Leo asked.

"Well, they're off the property, but they stopped on the road," Luther answered.

"Did the van have Oasis Flowers on it?" Leo asked.

"Yes!" Luther exclaimed.

"It was parked outside my house in Sacramento. They must have followed me. Or they already knew where I was going."

"And they're looking for me," murmured Tasha.

"Maybe it's about time you two told me what's really going on," Dutch said sourly.

Tasha glared at Leo. "I'll tell you the rest of my part, but Leo does have a part too. And he hasn't told me everything. Why don't you tell the story and this time, tell the whole thing."

Leo was quiet for a few minutes, and no one else stirred either. They were scared and even a bit angry. Just as Leo was about to open his mouth the lights came on. They all chimed with delight, but their delight passed as quickly as it came. They turned back to Leo to await his version of the story.

23

THE ROOM REMAINED SILENT WHEN LEO FINISHED TELLING THE STORY. He didn't leave anything out other than the names of his pals from East St Louis. No one was particularly surprised that Leo would have friends in the union who were capable of violence. What surprised them more was Tasha's story. She didn't look the part and her knowledge and demeanor gave her an air of a much higher social standing.

Dutch finally spoke. "Well, it seems that our visitors are after Tasha not Leo. Apparently Preacher Boy Ray has not given up on having Tasha work for him or he's just pissed that his goons got beat up. The question is what are we going to do about them."

"I'll leave," Tasha sighed. "I don't want to put any of the rest of you in harm's way."

"We'll go," Leo said, reaching for Tasha's hand. She let hers casually slip out of his grasp.

"Nowhere," Dutch finished firmly. "That asshole is going to find out he made a big mistake sending them here."

"Well, maybe Tasha could leave for awhile," Luther ventured timidly. "Just until those guys give up."

"Luther's right," Juniper said. "Some of us have more to lose by being involved."

Everyone gave Luther a sidelong glance, knowing what Juniper was inferring. He fumbled at trying to be helpful instead of a hindrance. "I think I know where she could go," Luther offered. "They probably wouldn't find her there, but I don't know how she could get there if they are waiting outside."

"Where?" Tasha asked.

"The hostel where I stayed when I was in San Francisco. We could call Monica and Jed. They'll help Tasha."

"But how will she get out of here without being seen?" Buster chimed in. "Leo can't take her, obviously. And Luther doesn't need to get involved with people that might cause him trouble."

Juniper sighed. "I guess it's up to me, then."

"Hold on, everyone," Dutch cut in. "Let's think this through. Anyone leaving here is going to look suspicious to them and get followed. I think we're better off having someone come and get her. She can hide in their car until the coast is clear on the road." Dutch got up from the table. "I'll make some calls."

"How long will I have to stay away?" Tasha asked.

Leo gave her a sad smile. "We'll just have to figure that out day by day. I will call you every day."

Tasha frowned. "I don't really like the idea of going south. It seems to me like a retreat from here. And a hostel seems too public. Why not go north instead? Why not—" Tasha brightened up—"why not Arcata? I can blend in with the students—" here she laughed a little — "well, at least I'll try, and check out the courses at Humboldt."

"I could call the union rep up there," Leo mused. "Maybe they could come get her under the guise of looking at Dutch's farm for organizing purposes."

"That might work," Juniper said. "Tasha could hide in the trunk of their car."

"Even if the union guys don't want to do it, we could ask one of the workers or dispensary owners," Leo added.

"Let's wait for Dutch to come back and see what he thinks," Tasha said.

Scarlett just gazed at Tasha, seemingly heartbroken at losing her confidant, and Homer was uncharacteristically quiet throughout this exchange. Finally he spoke. "I don't think it's fair to get anyone else involved. I think we need to deal with these clods head-on."

"How?" they all asked in unison.

"We'll scare 'em off. Let's put our thinking caps on. We'll come up with something."

"I have one idea," Scarlett said, surprising everyone. "Maybe Leo should drive away with a dummy sitting next to him and they'll follow him, thinking it's Tasha."

Buster laughed loudly. "And then what happens when they see it isn't? They'll just come right back."

"Or break Leo's neck," Juniper added.

"Using some kind of bait, though, is a good idea, Scarlett," Leo broke in. "Maybe I should call my East St Louis friends to meet me somewhere."

"Really?" Buster asked. "Are they going to do the job right this time?"

Leo exhaled loudly. "Honestly, I don't know exactly what my friends did to those guys. They may not have, uh, recovered that quickly."

"You mean they killed them?" Scarlett gasped.

"I didn't want to know."

"This sounds like it's becoming a vicious cycle," Buster sniffed.

That statement brought silence back into the room. They sat for several minutes, waiting for Dutch's return, until Juniper suddenly jumped up. "Hey, the electricity's back on, you know. We should be watching the news." They scrambled into the living room and Juniper pointed the remote at the TV. A commercial came on. "Well, that's good news already," she said. "The station is no longer on emergency mode."

The weatherman then came on and spoke of winds continuing out of the south and significant rain approaching by morning. Everyone in the room cheered. Next the newswoman reviewed the latest fire statistics, saying that the southern perimeter was controlled and the fire seventy percent contained. Everyone talked at once over the good news until Dutch appeared at the French doors. "I'm outta here," Dutch snapped. "I'm going to take care of this once and for all!"

Only Homer managed to find his voice. "How?"

"I've got ways." Dutch's grumbled. "It'll get done quickly, too." He left the room and everyone turned to Juniper.

"What's he gonna do?" Leo asked.

Juniper shifted uncomfortably. "Probably head to Alderpoint."

"Where's Alderpoint?" Luther asked.

"In the mountains. About twenty miles from here." Everyone looked to her for further explanation. "Let's just say that there are growers there that live by their own rules. It's also called Murder Mountain. It's no secret. There's even a documentary about it."

Leo sighed. "Well that's an ominous turn."

They heard the front door slam and Gypsy barking outside. Scarlett ran out and came back with the dog in tow. "Dutch just took off," she said.

"There's no cell service up there," Juniper murmured.

"Do you think this is a wise thing to do?" Luther whispered to Juniper.

She shrugged. "He must feel like he has to. I doubt it would be his first choice."

"Are they going to kill them?"

"Who knows what they'll do."

"There must be a reason it's known as Murder Mountain," Luther said.

"A lot of missing people . . . never an explanation . . ." Even at a whisper, everyone else caught the gist of Luther and Juniper's conversation. No one would look at each other.

"All this shit has made me tired," Buster finally announced. "I think I'll go to bed. Homer, you coming?"

"Damn right."

Luther turned to Tasha as the men left. "Do you think we still need to do guard duty outside?"

"Nah, I think we need sleep more than anything."

Leo smiled and tugged at her arm. "Let's go."

Luther noticed Scarlett giving Leo a piercing look and then locking eyes with Tasha. The two women exchanged barely perceptible nods and then Tasha got up and left with Leo. Luther looked at Scarlett, but she wouldn't look back. "Are you going to bed?" he finally asked her.

"No," she said, feigning indifference. "I think I'll stay down here for a while." She settled into the sofa and Gypsy got next to her while Minnie climbed into her lap.

"Okay then. See you in the morning." Luther stopped at Homer's door and listened. It was quiet, so he went to Juniper's room, tapped lightly on her door and opened it.

"Hey," she smiled and patted the bed next to her.

Luther climbed in and proceeded to tell her what had just happened with Scarlett and Tasha. "It was weird," he said.

"They have a strong connection."

"I know, but this was different . . . the way they looked at each other."

She shrugged. "It's not my concern. You are." She pulled him to her.

247

24

LUTHER WOKE UP TO THE SOUND OF RAIN PELTING THE ROOF. Juniper was already up and out of bed. He glanced at his phone and jumped up when he saw it was nine o'clock. When he got to the kitchen he saw the rest of the group lounging around the table, sipping coffee. "Well, look what the cat dragged in!" Buster chuckled.

"Hey, leave him alone," Scarlett snapped. "He's the one who's been pulling all-nighters."

"Just teasing," Buster replied.

"Homer," Luther asked. "Do we still need to go out and clear brush even though it's raining?"

"Nah, I think we're good. It's been raining for several hours."

Luther poured some coffee and looked around, noticing Dutch was missing. He looked at Juniper with raised eyebrows. She shook her head slightly and looked away. "Have you guys eaten?" he asked.

Juniper got up. "Just toast. The bread's on the counter. I have to go to the store now that the power's on. Why don't you all make up a list of what you want while I go get ready." She put a pad and pen on the table and left.

No one made a move. It was eerily quiet. Leo finally grabbed the pen and started writing. "Any requests?" he asked.

"No," Homer said. "Juniper won't buy the things I ask for, anyway."

"Same here," Buster said. "Just let her get the essentials."

"I wish I could go myself," Tasha said.

"You and I aren't going anywhere until those punks are out of here," Leo replied.

Tasha sighed. "I'm sorry, guys, for bringing all this crap down on you."

"We've all brought crap to the table," Homer replied. Tasha hugged him and kissed him on the cheek. "Aw shucks," he teased.

"Hey Scarlett, where's Gypsy? Does she need to go out?" Tasha asked.

"She's already out."

"She's probably pretty wet then." Tasha gave her a significant smile. "Maybe we can go get her and dry her off?"

Luther looked at Leo, but he seemed oblivious. He glanced at Buster and Homer to see if they had noticed anything unusual, but they were busy joking with each other. He ate his toast quickly and went looking for Juniper. He glanced at the front door as he passed and saw Tasha and Scarlett toweling off Gypsy while deep in conversation. Then Tasha kissed Scarlett on the lips and whispered in her ear. He rushed off to find Juniper and share the gossip, laughing at himself for acting like a teenage girl. He found Juniper grabbing the hemp bags from the kitchen for the groceries.

"Do you want to come with me?" Juniper asked before he had a chance to open his mouth.

"Yeah! Sure! But I was right," he gushed.

"Right about what?"

"Tasha and Scarlett. I saw them kissing, on the lips."

"Yeah . . . so?"

"You knew? What about Leo?"

"What do you mean?"

Luther frowned. "I thought Tasha and Leo were together."

Juniper laughed. "So what? Tasha's probably bi."

"Bi?" Luther shook his head.

"Bisexual?" Juniper looked at him incredulously. "You never heard of anyone being bisexual?"

"Yeah, I guess so, but I don't think Scarlett's too happy about sharing."

Juniper shrugged. "Not my business." They went back to the kitchen. Leo was alone at the table, on the phone. He handed Juniper the list he had made and a twenty-dollar bill. Luther thought it interesting that she took his money this time. "I'll meet you at the car," she said. "I'll be right there."

The rain was still coming down heavily when Luther got outside. He ran to the car and got in the driver's seat to wait for Juniper. He wanted to familiarize himself with a different vehicle and that made him think about what was in the back of the truck. The marijuana was in plastic containers, but he worried about it getting wet. He got out of the car to check and ran toward the truck. He noticed some dark figures lurking just outside the fence. They were in camouflage outfits and were carrying shotguns on their backs. Luther turned around and ran back to the car.

"Where were you?" Juniper asked when Luther slipped into the passenger seat.

"I was going to check on the pot in the back of the truck. You know, make sure it was dry. There were these guys, dressed in camouflage, right outside the fence. They had guns."

Juniper nodded. "Were they near the gate?"

"No, down the road."

"Okay. Then I guess it's safe to go to town."

"What? You're not concerned?"

"They're on our side."

"They're from Alderpoint?"

"Yeah. Now let's get out of here." She started the engine and drove off.

"And where were you?" Luther asked.

"I wanted to check on Homer."

"Is he okay?"

"Yeah, he and Buster are fine. You were right, though, about Scarlett. She's not so good."

"Did you talk to her?"

"No, I just heard her crying and Tasha talking to her," Juniper answered.

"Are you worried about her?"

"Of course. Well, she is fragile and just off drugs."

"Wasn't she forced to take drugs? I mean, why would she necessarily turn to them?"

"I don't really know what she'll do, Luther. I'm no rehab therapist. Hopefully things will work out between her and Tasha and it won't be an issue." Juniper took a deep breath.

As the gate opened and they drove through, they heard gunshots down the road. "Oh shit!" Luther yelled.

Juniper sped off in the opposite direction. As the car gained speed the wipers couldn't keep up with the pouring rain. "I can't see a fucking thing!" Suddenly she was on an abrupt curve. She twisted the steering wheel and the car fishtailed, and then it was strangely silent as the car went airborne. It hurled sideways off the road, clipped a tree and went nose first down an embankment. The brushing of twigs became the crashing of branches and the screech of metal as the car bore back down to earth. The roar of reality returned as the air bags exploded and the car ground to a halt.

"Jesus!" Luther exhaled, pushing the deflating bags out of the way. "Are you okay?"

"I'm okay. You?"

"Yeah. What happened?"

Juniper shook her head. "Hydroplaned, I guess. Like walking on water."

"Huh? What are these things?" he demanded, batting at the limp fabric all around him.

"Airbags," She answered.

"Is the car okay?"

"We'll soon find out." She put it in reverse and tried to back up, but the wheels just spun.

"Let me push," Luther said opening the door.

"You can't do it alone. We can call Leo, Tasha and Scarlett to come down and help."

"And have those freaks down the road on top of them in no time. What makes you think I can't do it alone?"

"It's a ton of metal and it's stuck in the mud."

"Watch me!" Luther demanded, wired on adrenaline.

"Fine. Don't believe me. Go ahead and try." Luther got out, went to the dented hood and leaned on it, pushing with all his might as Juniper halfheartedly applied some gas. His only reward was the sloppy whine of tires spinning in mud. Juniper started laughing and that just made him persist even more. Juniper stuck her head out the window. "Okay he-man. You better stop before you give yourself a hernia."

Luther took a deep breath and threw all his weight against the car. It jostled slightly, causing Juniper to tap the gas again. The car lurched backwards into firmer ground, and Juniper started backing slowly and steadily while Luther chased her screaming with joy. Juniper turned the car around and Luther got in. "Well?" he grinned. She kissed him.

"You better not have hurt yourself," she breathed on his sweaty, rain-soaked face.

The rain had let up slightly by the time they got back to the farm. They saw Dutch's car parked in front and both of them breathed a sigh of relief. They hadn't spoken anymore about the gunshot or the Alderpoint outlaws, but they had both been worried. He was sitting in the kitchen with Leo when they walked in with the groceries. "Good morning," he said, smiling at Luther and Juniper. "It's all taken care of."

Although Luther was dying to know what happened, he knew better than to ask. "Hey Juniper, tell these guys how strong I am," Luther teased.

Juniper laughed. "We hydroplaned and landed on an embankment in the mud. Mr. Macho Man here pushed the car all by himself to free us." Luther grinned. Leo seemed less than impressed, but Dutch gave him a high-five. "Well, you might reconsider the high-five after you see the car," Juniper said.

Dutch grinned at Luther. "You weren't driving the car, were you?"

"No sir!"

Dutch looked back at Juniper slyly. "Good thing."

Homer and Buster arrived at that moment. "Hey, Dutch. What was all that racket earlier this morning?" Homer asked. "That you shooting off guns?"

"What noise?" Dutch deflected. "I just got back. How ya feeling, Homer?"

"I'm okay."

"How's the music festival coming?" Buster asked.

"We've got some good acts coming in. It'll be great."

"Who you got coming?"

"You and Leo come back into the music room with me. We've got some more planning to do." Dutch got up and Buster and Leo followed him out.

Homer sat down. "Did you bring me any surprises?" Juniper reached into one of the bags and took out a bag of chips. "You're a doll. Want some, Luther?"

"Not now, maybe later."

"There won't be any later." Homer winked. "Hey, are we going down to the barn today?"

"I don't know. I wanted to talk to Dutch to ask him what else he wants me to do. I mean us." Luther glanced at Juniper. "You think I can interrupt them for a minute?"

"You've got to stop being afraid of Dutch."

Luther frowned. "Trusting people doesn't come easily to me."

She rubbed his back. "Go ahead and knock. I'm sure it's fine."

Luther went to the music room and knocked. "Dutch? I just want to know what else you want me to do in the barn?"

"Come on in," Dutch answered.

Luther went in tentatively. Buster had his guitar and played softly while Leo sat at the computer. "Are we still planning on getting animals?" Luther asked.

"Why wouldn't we?" Dutch replied.

"I thought maybe with the fire and the festival that you may have changed your mind."

"Not at all. In fact, I've heard there are some animals displaced by the fire and need a place to go. Is the barn usable as is?"

"I guess."

"As long as it's safe and secure."

"Then it's probably ready, but I'll go down when the rain lets up a little more."

"Okay," Dutch nodded. "I'll find out about getting the animals delivered here."

"What kind of animals are they?" Buster asked.

"Not sure. Goats, horses, chickens, cows. I'll make some calls in a little while. I need to finish up with Leo first."

Luther slipped out and ran into Tasha in the hallway. "Is Leo in there?" she asked.

"Yeah, he and Dutch are working on the music festival plans." He noticed how stressed she looked. "He said it's all under control. I don't think you have anything else to worry about."

She nodded, but it didn't seem to relieve her. "Where's Juniper?" she asked.

"In the kitchen last I knew."

Tasha went to the kitchen and Luther decided to leave those two alone to talk. He went to shower and maybe even lay down for a spell. He heard Scarlett crying as he walked by her room and debated about knocking. Maybe she wanted someone's ear who wasn't directly involved with the love triangle that seemed to be tearing her apart. She can only tell him to go away. He knocked gently. "Yeah?" Scarlett said.

"It's Luther. You okay?"

"Come on in."

Luther opened the door timidly. "Can I help?"

"I don't think so. The ball's in Tasha's court." She looked into his eyes. "You didn't know did you?"

Luther thought it wise to play dumb. "Know what?"

"Tasha's a lesbian. So am I."

"But she was a call girl."

"Prostitution has nothing to do with lovemaking. It's just mechanical sex. It's a game. Same as what I had to do."

"What about Leo?"

"He was a way out. Don't judge her. She had to."

"I get it. Leo doesn't know, though does he?"

Scarlett shook her head. "She has to tell him."

"Then why are you crying? She's chosen you over him."

She sighed. "Because until I'm sure — until he's gone. Oh, I've got to regain my soul and spirit somehow."

"You're smart, Scarlett. And strong."

"Thanks, Luther." She hugged him.

Luther got up to leave. "Where are Gypsy and Minnie?"

"Minnie could be anywhere. Gypsy's probably in the living room on the sofa. She likes to be comfortable."

"Do you want me to check?" he asked.

"Nah. She'll come find me when she's hungry or needs to go out. She's a smart puppy. She knows the weather isn't conducive to playing outside."

Luther showered and looked out his window. The rain had let up enough to make a walk down to the barn pleasant. He went to the kitchen first to find Homer, but no one was there. He was reluctant to go to the barn by himself. He really had no idea what it had to look like to be ready for animals. But hey, he had pushed a two-ton car out of mud. How hard could it be to make a barn livable for animals?

He opened the front door to leave when Leo came storming out of the living room. Luther watched him rush down the hall and then went into the living room. Tasha sat on the sofa, petting Gypsy. She looked up at him and shrugged sheepishly. "He says he's going to leave."

"Are you okay with that?" Luther asked.

"It's fine with me. I just hope it doesn't leave Dutch in a lurch."

"Dutch is resourceful and we can all help," Luther replied. "Hey, have you seen Homer?"

"He was in the kitchen with Juniper."

"No one's there now. I need some help getting the barn ready. I guess Dutch is going to take in some animals that were displaced by the fire."

"Oh cool! I'll help you."

Luther smiled. Tasha could actually do some work. "That would be great."

"Maybe Scarlett will want to help too. I'll go ask her and meet you down there."

"Okay. I'll see if Dutch has anything specific he wants done." Luther knocked quietly on the music room door.

"Who is it?" Dutch asked.

"Luther." He heard Dutch unlock the door and open it slightly. "Can I come in?"

"That's why I opened the door."

Luther entered the room and saw Dutch sitting on a stool playing a very old shabby guitar. "Is that yours?" Luther asked.

Dutch smiled. "Yes."

"It doesn't look like your other ones."

"I don't take it out much to play. I've had it a long time."

"Is it your first?" Luther asked.

"Let's just say it's very special. Now, what did you want?"

"Oh, I'm going down to the barn. Tasha is going to help me. Is there anything else you want me to do there?"

"I'll come down in a bit."

Luther nodded and left. It was obvious that Dutch wanted to be alone to play that crappy guitar, for whatever reason. He walked down to the barn, feeling good about getting back on track. The fire and those punks were in the past. The future was looking good for everyone on the farm . . . except Leo.

25

LUTHER WAS CLEANING OUT A STALL WHEN TASHA SHOWED UP WITH SCARLETT AND GYPSY IN TOW. "Sorry it took so long, but I felt that I had to talk to Dutch about what happened," Tasha said.

"What did he say?" Luther asked.

"He said my relationship with Leo had nothing to do with their business arrangement and that I shouldn't worry about it — he'd talk to him. He was real mellow about it."

"We could all learn from him," Luther responded.

"Maybe it comes from all those years of smoking pot," Scarlett giggled.

Luther thought that was the first time he had ever seen her laugh or even smile, and he smiled back at her. "Did he say when he'd be coming down?" he asked Tasha.

"He said he'd be down after he talks to Leo."

Tasha and Scarlett started helping Luther with the cleanup and they got several more stalls done by the time Dutch appeared. "Luther, I need some help picking up the animals."

"Uh, okay, but is the barn ready for them?"

Dutch glanced around. "It's good enough. Tasha, you and Scarlett talk to Juniper and round up some rope and feed bins. You might need to go to the feed store. Juniper knows what to do. The store's in Redway. She can direct you."

"I'm getting to know Redway quite well." Tasha winked at Luther and took Scarlett's arm. "Let's go."

Luther was happy to have Dutch alone for once. He had so many things he wanted to ask him, but he didn't know how to start. Finally he brought up the pot in the truck. "Are we just going to leave the pot in the back of the pick-up for now?"

"Maybe you can unload it and put it back after we get the animals situated."

More silence as Luther got up the nerve to ask about Leo and the music festival. "So did Leo leave?"

"For now. He's pissed, understandably. Nobody likes being used."

"He sure looked like he was in love with her."

"Yeah."

"Will you be able to organize the music festival without him?" Luther asked.

Dutch grinned. "I'm resourceful."

"Is he going back to union organizing?"

Dutch laughed. "How the hell should I know? I didn't ask. He'll be fine. He doesn't need us. He was only here because of Tasha."

That statement really hit home. Dutch was right. Leo didn't need the farm, but the rest of them did. It was a sanctuary for all of them. Dutch noticed his pensive mood and glanced over at him. Luther smiled back. "Thank you."

Dutch nodded. "Thank you as well. You're proving to be a good worker."

Luther hoped he meant it. They drove perhaps a dozen miles in silence and arrived at a huge warehouse in a clearing in the middle of nowhere. It looked like part of an abandoned lumber camp that had been sitting empty for many years. But surrounding the building was a huge assortment of animals: cows, horses, goats, dogs, and sheep. They walked inside the building and found it populated with chickens. A woman approached them. "Hi, you must be Dutch. I'm Madeline."

Dutch and Madeline shook hands. "This is Luther."

"Howdy Luther. So, how many can you take?"

"Is this temporary until the fire victims find their animals and have a place to put them?" Dutch asked.

"We don't know about a lot of them. Some we know need permanent homes," Madeline answered.

"I'd like to take ones that need permanent homes."

"Okay. Let Felix know. He's outside with the truck. There's just some paperwork to sign."

Dutch turned to Luther. "Would you go outside and talk to Felix while I sign the papers?"

"Sure, but what kind and how many?"

"What's available?" Dutch asked Madeline.

"Felix knows the details better than I do. Several people have come by looking for animals already today, so I'm behind on the paperwork."

Luther gave Dutch an anxious look. "But what do *you* want?"

"Just make sure we get some that'll give us milk and eggs – the rest don't matter," Dutch replied.

Luther went outside, shaking his head. How was this ghetto child supposed to know anything about farm animals? He found Felix by the truck and introduced himself. "My boss wants to keep the animals permanently. And he wants ones that give milk and eggs for sure and others too, I guess," Luther added tentatively.

Felix scoffed. "How would I know which ones are producing? They're all freaked out by the fire anyway. Let's just try to load up as many females as we can without upsetting everyone."

Luther panicked. Did Felix expect him to know how to get them into the truck? Thankfully Felix took a stick and rounded up a cow and a mare, which seemed inseparable from a burro. Luther looked around helplessly. "Uh, should I go get some chickens?" he finally asked.

"Yeah, you do that."

Luther happily went back into the warehouse and found Dutch and Madeline filling out forms. "How should we bring the chickens?" he asked, trying to sound like he knew what he was talking about.

"I'll get a crate," Madeline said and went to a corner of the warehouse.

About a half hour later, Felix had the truck full and Dutch and Luther were back on the road toward the farm. "Homer's going to be excited," Dutch said.

"Does he know you went to get the animals today?"

"Nah. It'll be a surprise." Dutch started singing "Old McDonald Had A Farm."

"Maybe you and Buster could write a new song," Luther murmured. Dutch laughed heartily.

They got to the farm and Dutch led the truck to the barn. Felix opened the back of the truck and stood aside. "I just drive the truck. They're yours now."

Luther looked at Dutch, waiting for him to make a move. "Go ahead, Luther," Dutch smiled at Luther's panic-stricken face. "Bring them out."

Luther went inside the truck gingerly. He tried to remember what Juniper had done with Zorba. Should he hold on to their neck and guide them out? He was afraid they'd bite him or kick him, but he couldn't figure out any other way. He took the mare's neck and gently turned it towards the door. She turned around and walked down the ramp and to Luther's happy surprise, the other animals followed. He grinned at Dutch and shrugged. "That was easy."

"Put the chickens inside one of the stalls," Dutch said. "I forgot about needing a chicken house. Go find Homer and bring him down. You and he can go about building one tomorrow morning."

Luther ran up to the house and found the whole gang in the living room. "The animals are here," he said breathlessly.

"No shit!" Buster said.

Homer got up. "Let's go."

They all got up and trekked down to the barn. The rain had stopped and it was just getting dark. "Look at that!" Scarlett shouted, pointing to the animals grazing alongside the path. "This is going to be great!"

"Dutch wants us to build a chicken coop tomorrow," Luther told Homer.

"Where are the chickens now?" Homer asked. "Are they safe from the rest of these critters?"

"They're in one of the stalls. I guess they're safe as long as the animals stay outside."

"As long as raccoons can't get in," Homer muttered. "Make sure that stall is secure from the outside and nothing can squeeze in."

They fawned over the animals for a few minutes until Juniper said she needed to make dinner and the others agreed that it was getting awfully dark. They trudged back to the house and chattered happily through the dinner hour. They were like excited little children, eagerly wishing for morning so they could play with the animals again.

They awoke to a bright sunny day and a picture-perfect start to a new era at the farm. All hands were on deck. By one o'clock the chicken coop was built; the feeding stations were in place for the cows, goats, and sheep in the pasture; the horses were in stalls and introduced to Zorba who had joined them in a new home; Buster had written a song; and Dutch was on the phone working on the next project: the music festival. Minnie installed herself as the barn's pest warden and made it her new go-to place for hunting. Gypsy was not as adventurous, preferring to bark at the animals rather than go after them. She much preferred the comfortable life in the house, being pampered in general and spoiled by Scarlett in particular.

Life at the farm was idyllic all winter as they learned how to milk the cows and goats. They bought a loom and Scarlett made it her vocation to learn to weave and knit. Tasha went about planning and tending the garden and orchards of fruits and vegetables. Juniper took over the pot business, although on a much smaller scale, while Homer bossed everyone around. Nobody cared, though, since he had experience in almost every single aspect of farming. Buster surprised Dutch at his ability to help with the planning of the music festival, and the two of them had secured a great line-up of musicians.

Luther was everyone's right hand man. He loved it because it gave him a chance to learn

every aspect of running the farm including
keeping up with the feed and hardware required.
He had passed the driving test with flying colors
and was the first to volunteer for errand running.
He had also developed an affinity for horses and
that pleased him no end since it gave him another
way to spend more time with Juniper.

26

DUTCH AND BUSTER SPENT MOST OF THEIR TIME IN THE MUSIC ROOM WHILE EVERYONE ELSE BUSIED THEMSELVES AROUND THE FARM. Everyone was in on an early planning meeting and they voted on calling the festival *Blues at The Last Resort*. Once word got out tickets started selling fast. Wavy Gravy's Hog Farm was only about an hour away and he and Dutch had crossed paths many times in the last forty years. Wavy had put on many music festivals so he was an enormous help. And best of all, he had agreed to emcee. Every musician who had signed up was performing gratis so all the proceeds could go to the Bull Creek fire victims, both human and animal. Luther, Juniper, Tasha, and Scarlett built the stage under Homer's supervision, so they saved on construction costs. The sound system crew donated their time and skills, so Dutch only had to pay for the equipment rental itself. Security would be taken care of by Wavy's Hog

Farm. The Hog Farm had done security for Woodstock fifty years ago. They knew their way around music festivals. Wavy loaned Dutch a tent for first aid and a tent to use as a dressing room. Several catering trucks in the area were going to provide food; a local brewery was taking care of beer; and the portable bathrooms were ordered. The last piece of the pie was getting a permit, but since it was private property, only an alcohol one was needed.

The line up was stellar. Every musician was over the age of sixty-five and many of the roadies traveling with them had retired but came back just to help with this festival. It would be a happy reunion for many of them. As a one-day affair, Dutch could keep the number of performers down to a comfortable number, although he had heard from several of his musician pals that they were coming just to be in the audience and to donate. Best of all, ticket sales were brisk and it looked like they were going to sell out.

About a week before the festival was to take place, after breakfast and the rest of the gang had gone outside to work, Buster and Dutch sat in the music room, putting the final touches on the parking map.

"Looks like clear sailing from here," Dutch said, "Unless we're hit with a crosswind."

"We will be, but there ain't a thing we can do about it until it happens," Buster answered. "Let's take a break and make some music ourselves."

Dutch sat quietly for a moment, staring out the window while Buster took out his guitar and started picking. Dutch finally got up and went to a door that appeared to be a closet. He put in a code and opened the door, but there was another door directly behind it. Buster looked up curiously and watched Dutch take out a key and open the second door and walked through it, shutting the door behind him.

"What the hell?" Buster muttered to himself. Dutch came out of the second door and then the first door, holding an old, beat-up guitar. "Whatcha got there, Dutch?" Dutch didn't answer, but sat down next to Buster and started to tune it. "That's one crappy-looking guitar. Is that the one you learned to play on or something?" Buster asked.

"You gotta promise me something, Buster. If I tell you about this guitar, you can't tell a soul. You'd be the first person I ever told. And I want you to be the last until I decide what I'm going to do with it."

"Jesus, Dutch, what is this? Yeah, you can trust me."

"Buster, I really mean this. I'm not kidding around." Dutch stared hard into Buster's eyes.

"I promise, man. Not a word."

Dutch took a deep breath and played the beginning riff to "Crossroads." He kept gazing into Buster's eyes as he played. When he stopped, he smiled at Buster. "Recognize that riff?"

"Yeah, of course."

"I was raised in southern California and when I was a teenager, learning the guitar and playing in high school garage bands, I met a man." He stopped and played a few notes.

"And? Who was he?" Buster asked.

"Isaiah Zimmerman."

"Ike The Blues man?"

"Yup."

"You met him in Los Angeles?"

"Yeah, after he moved to Compton from Mississippi."

"When was that?" Buster asked.

"Oh, in sixty-five, I think. He died in sixty-seven."

"He's the one who played with Robert Johnson," Buster mused. "I think they wrote a couple of songs together."

Dutch kept strumming his guitar for quite awhile. "You know he was actually Robert Johnson's teacher?" Dutch finally said.

Buster laughed. "You mean Johnson didn't actually make a deal with the devil?"

Dutch smiled. "Ike told me that story started because they used to practice together at a cemetery."

"Why the hell did he move to California?"

"He never told me why. He was a minister when I met him. Maybe he had kids there or something. We never talked much about our personal lives."

"You played with him?"

Dutch nodded. "Some. Mostly he talked and I listened."

They were quiet for several minutes, both of them mindlessly strumming the evolution of the blues. "So that's what you don't want me to tell anyone? That you met Ike Zimmerman?" Buster finally asked.

"No." Dutch paused and took a breath. "You know there are a lot of stories about what happened to Robert Johnson's guitar?"

"I know. And they never proved any of them." Buster's eyes widened. "Hold it — you telling me that guitar you're playing —"

"It is," Dutch interrupted. "Ike sold it to me. He desperately needed money and I had just signed with a label. He had no idea how much it would be worth."

"Lord almighty!" Buster exhaled and sat back in his chair. "You sure it's the real thing?"

Dutch showed Buster the back of the guitar with RL Johnson's signature scratched into it. "It's a Kalamazoo KG-14. I had it authenticated some years ago. I've got papers from three different appraisers. He used the initials RL when he lived with the Zimmermans. Not everyone knows that."

"What do they say is its value?"

"At least a million."

"Well butter my biscuit!"

"Not a word, Buster. No one, and I mean no one, knows except the appraisers and they signed nondisclosure papers."

"I promise Dutch. But what are you gonna do with it?"

"I haven't decided for sure, yet. Donate it to the Musical Instrument Museum in Phoenix, I think."

"What? You don't want to sell it?"

"Buster, I really don't need all that money. I'm happy with what I got. If I sell it, it would be to donate the proceeds anyway." Dutch handed it to Buster. "It's a pretty lousy guitar, actually. Probably cost about ten dollars in the thirties."

Buster strummed it and laughed. "You're not kidding." He handed it back to Dutch. "So, why are you telling me this secret? Why now? Why me?"

"That fire got me thinking about our mortality. Could happen anytime. I just wanted someone else to know about the guitar and you're the only one here who would really appreciate its history."

"But I'll go before you," Buster replied.

Dutch smiled and shrugged. "One never knows, does one?"

"Billie Holiday's signature song." Buster picked up his guitar and started playing the song. "You must have been nervous as a cat in a room full of rocking chairs when that fire came so close. Did you take the guitar with you?"

"I did."

"Where'd you go anyway without anyone seeing the guitar?" Buster asked.

"If I hadn't told you whose guitar this was, would you think it was worth anything?" Dutch answered with a sly smile.

Buster laughed. "I guess you're right."

"Look at the cracks in the front and how bowed the neck is," Dutch said. "Even the tuning machines don't turn freely anymore."

"You wouldn't want to fix it up anyway. It would lose a lot of value."

"I'm not looking to play it."

Buster got serious. "You never told Juniper or anybody about this guitar?"

Dutch shook his head. "Never needed to. The fire brought it home to me that maybe somebody else needed to know. Just in case something ever happened to me."

"You have it insured though, right?"

"Yeah, but it isn't the monetary value that makes it special."

Buster nodded. "You gonna give me that code and a key? I mean, if it's about getting it when you're not here."

"Not now. It's more that I wanted someone to know it was here and where it was."

"I get it," Buster said. Dutch rose and put the guitar back, closing and locking the doors behind him. "Thanks, Dutch. For trusting me."

Dutch rested his hand on Buster's shoulder. "Let's go see how the others are doing."

27

HOMER'S HEALTH DECLINED AS THE DAY OF THE MUSIC FESTIVAL APPROACHED. There was a vaping crisis across the country where people were getting sick, even dying. It scared Homer, even though it was about specific vape pens that people were buying, nothing to do with what Dutch provided for him. There was nothing Dutch could say to change his mind about it. Juniper baked some cookies and brownies with the Kobain Kush, but the edibles didn't work as well as the vape pipe for Homer. He was spending more and more time in bed and refused to go to a doctor or take any of the medicine he had received in the past. The tremors grew worse and became continual. Then memory issues began and finally hallucinations.

Luther scraped another batch of brownie batter from the sides of the bowl with a spatula. Juniper leaned in, using the opportunity to teach Luther some cooking skills. She looked down at the rich chocolaty mess and sighed. "I just don't think there is any recipe that will deliver the goods."

"We've got to keep trying," Luther said quietly, dipping his finger into the batter and tasting it.

"I know. I'm not giving up." Juniper choked. Luther let the spatula slide into the batter as he put his arms around her. Her body relaxed against his and a flood of tears came.

Tasha and Scarlett burst into the kitchen with Gypsy at their heels. "We need to go to the feed store. You guys want anything?" Tasha exclaimed. "Oh," she softened. "Everything okay, Juniper?"

Juniper pulled away from Luther. "I'm fine." She fished the spatula out of the batter and started mixing again.

Tasha smiled understandingly at Luther and pulled Scarlett away. "Call if you think of anything you need," she said leaving the kitchen.

"Should I go check on Homer?" Luther asked Juniper.

"Sure."

Luther knocked softly on Homer's door. "Homer? You in here?" He heard a grunt and opened the door. "How ya doin'? Can I get you anything?"

"Battroo."

"Battroo?" Luther asked. Homer's face got red and he pointed his trembling hand toward the door. "Oh, bathroom?" Homer nodded. Luther reached under Homer's arms to try and pull his shaking body up. He got him sitting but as soon as Homer tried to stand, his legs buckled.

Homer scrunched his face in anger and spit as he stammered, "C-c-cat wah."

"Oh man, Homer, I'm so sorry you're going through this." Luther sighed. "Juniper's baking a new recipe for you, but she'd rather you went back to vaping, or at least putting the tincture under your tongue. She said vaping's the best."

Homer took a deep breath and said as he shook his head, "no walk."

"I know, Homer. Luther pulled him into a standing position and fairly dragged him into the bathroom. "You need a wheelchair, Homer." Homer hung his head further down but did not protest.

The whole trip to the bathroom was exhausting for both of them. Luther had Homer sitting upright on the bed, with his arm around his shoulder for support. Homer's shaking grew very rhythmic, like weeping, but there was no noise, no tears. Finally Homer said very slowly, very clearly," Vape."

"Yes, Homer," Luther cried, squeezing him. "Absolutely." He placed Homer's hands on his knees in hopes he'd remained balanced and got up to go get Juniper, only to run into her at the bedroom door with a plate of brownies in her hand. "Homer says he'll go back to vaping."

Juniper smiled. "Oh good. I'll get his pipe."

"He's also willing to get a wheelchair."

"I'll call Tasha and she can pick one up at the Medical Supply store in Garberville," Juniper replied, happy to be in control again. "I'll get Dutch to give the store his credit card number," she added from the hall.

Luther looked over at Homer, listing on the bed and saw the frown. He wanted to say something comforting, but didn't know what to say. They sat in silence, waiting for Juniper to return with the pipe. She finally did and handed Homer the pipe. His hand shook uncontrollably and Luther and Juniper glanced at each other, wondering if they should hold the pipe for him. But they knew somehow that he needed to get the pipe up to his lips himself. He finally did and took a long drag. "Hey, Homer, you know Jed and Monica are coming to the music festival," Luther said a little too cheerfully. "They'll be so happy to see you." Homer managed a crooked smile.

"Where's your iPod?" Juniper asked. Homer pointed to his night table. His hand was still shaking, but less. She picked it up and saw that it was out of juice. She opened her mouth to scold him for not keeping it charged, but ended up just quietly plugging it in. "Maybe you need to see a doctor," she said tentatively.

"No!" Homer bellowed. Juniper sighed loudly.

"Maybe there's some new thing that could help," Luther added.

Homer shook his head, lay down and closed his eyes. Luther and Juniper looked at each other and stood to leave. "Tanks," Homer whispered. Juniper wiped a tear away as they left the room and shut the door.

"Is this it?" Luther asked when they got back to the kitchen.

"It appears to be the last stage of the disease," she answered, her voice cracking. "Dutch has been researching online and consulting with a doctor — as much good as that does without seeing the patient."

"Well," Luther hesitated, "we knew this would happen eventually."

"Doesn't make it any easier."

"I know. I'm glad Jed and Monica will be here soon before it gets ugly."

"It's already ugly."

"It's real life, Juniper."

"Yeah, well, I don't have to like it." She left the kitchen.

Luther went outside to check the stage and was almost run over by Tasha pushing the wheelchair, yelling and laughing. "Oh, sorry Luther. Didn't see you coming out the door," Scarlett said as she jumped out of the seat. Gypsy was barking and running around in circles. It was a cheerful scene and it took Luther out of his gloomy mood.

"Is Homer up so we can bring him the chair?"

"I think he's sleeping. He finally vaped and it helped."

"Oh good. Well, here's the chair," Samantha replied. "We're going to feed the animals."

"I'll come too." Luther joined in with their playfulness and the trio ran down to the barn and pastures.

Later Tasha and Scarlett helped Juniper in the kitchen while Luther got Homer into the wheelchair. Buster and Dutch arrived to complete the family dinner. The conversation was stilted since no one knew what to say about the wheelchair. Homer looked down at his plate. The table around him was splattered with food, and obviously not much had reached his mouth. "Homer, what do you want us to do?" Juniper asked, her voice shrill with emotion. "Do you want to eat more? Do you want us to feed you? We want to help but we don't know how." Homer did not respond.

Dutch got up and went to the kitchen counter. He took out some peanut butter and jelly and slapped a sandwich together. He silently handed the sandwich to Homer's shaking hand and went back to his seat. Homer managed to get the sandwich to his mouth and took a bite. They all breathed a sigh of relief and the conversation became more lively and relaxed.

28

IT WAS FRIDAY, THE DAY BEFORE THE FESTIVAL, AND THE FARM HAD MORPHED INTO A MADHOUSE. The sound crew had arrived early in the morning for set up and Wavy Gravy had come around to help supervise them. Tasha and Scarlett moved the animals to a pasture far from the music, while Luther and Dutch ran around making sure the construction was safe, the parking area was cordoned off, and the catering trucks, the brewery, and the portable toilets were set up properly. Juniper worked the phones, making sure the musicians and their crews were en route. She also collaborated with the Benbow Inn to make sure their rooms and meals were taken care of.

Buster babysat Homer who was becoming more and more debilitated and depressed. Dutch had tried five different strains, but so far none had been working well, even with the vape pipe. "You gonna be able to do the festival, Homer?" Buster asked as he made him a baloney sandwich. Juniper had broken down and bought Homer anything he could eat with his hands, no matter how unhealthy.

"Gotta."

"Man, don't you think a doctor would help? Maybe some pills, even if they have side effects, would be better than this."

Homer shook his head. "No mo."

"No more what?" Buster asked. Homer sighed and Buster nodded as he patted Homer's shoulder. Buster let him eat his sandwich in peace before asking him, "Do you want to go out and see the action?"

"K." Buster wheeled Homer outside just as Luther approached the house while talking on his phone.

Luther put the phone away and called out, "Jed and Monica are here. I just gave them the code to open the gate. They'll be here in a minute."

Homer smiled and Buster set the brake on the wheelchair and awaited their arrival. Soon a car drove up and the doors opened as soon as it stopped. "Homer!" Jed said as he rushed toward him.

Luther pulled Monica aside and spoke in low tones. "He's really bad. The pot isn't working anymore. He can't walk and he slurs his words."

"Sounds like it's time to try something new," Monica frowned.

"Dutch has some other ideas he wants to try, but he hasn't had time lately because of the festival."

"I'll make some calls once we settle in," she said. "I think I can sniff out some experimental treatments, too. She adjusted her pensive look into a forced smile and turned toward Homer. She approached him and bent down to give him a big hug. "Oh, we've missed you." She used the gesture as a guise to wipe away tears she didn't want him to see.

Homer sniffled. "Me too."

Luther hugged them both. "This is Buster. I told you about him."

Jed shook Buster's hand. "You didn't need to tell me about him. I knew him when I was just a kid. Great to meet you. This is my wife, Monica."

"Hi Buster. This is an honor."

"Buster grinned. "You ain't seen nothing yet! Wait 'til you meet the cats playing here tomorrow. Way more famous than me."

"Oh, I don't know. Your records were a staple in my house growing up," she answered.

"Well, thank you. Homer and I were just going to take a spin around and see what's happening. You wanna come?"

"Sure," Jed said looking at Monica.

"Let's go find Dutch. I know he wants to see you guys too," Luther said.

Luther took the handles from Buster and started pushing Homer. "Dutch is over by the parking area and it's a tough road," he explained to Buster.

"I walk," Homer said as he tried to get out of the wheelchair.

"Homer!" Buster admonished. "You can't."

Homer turned to Luther. "Get w-w-walker?"

Luther looked at Buster and shrugged. "Okay. I'll be right back." Luther went in the house.

Jed and Buster each took an arm and helped Homer stand. "Are you sure, Homer?" Monica asked. "Luther said it's a tough road."

Homer didn't answer but pulled his arms out of Jed and Buster's grasp. He teetered but then was able to stand. He smiled at them. Luther came running back with Homer's walker in his hand. "Here you go," Luther said as he placed the walker in front of Homer.

Homer took a tentative step or two, and then with a determined look on his face, started walking. They all followed and although it was slow going, Homer managed to walk down the road while Luther took up the rear with the empty wheelchair. They found Dutch talking to the Honey Pot guy setting up the chemical toilets. When he saw the group coming toward him, he grinned and walked over. "You're here," he said to Jed and Monica and hugged them. "And you're walking," he said to a smiling Homer. "Does Juniper know you're here?"

"Not yet," Luther said. "They haven't been inside yet."

"You want to see the stage?" Dutch asked. "Come on, I want to introduce you to Wavy too."

"Wavy?" Monica asked.

"Wavy Gravy."

"I've heard the name. Was he a musician?" she replied. "At Woodstock?"

"Yeah, but also a peace activist. You ever heard of the Hog Farm?"

"Sure. Wasn't that a commune?"

"Wavy started it years ago and it's still going. He owns the Black Oak Ranch down in Laytonville and he's put on lots of music festivals. He's been helping me along with the Hog Farm crew and they're going to do the security. He also hosts a circus and performing arts camp every summer at his ranch called Camp Winnarainbow. All the proceeds go to charity."

"He sounds like a great guy," Monica said.

"One of the best. Where did Jed and Luther go?" he asked as he looked around.

"They're hanging back with Homer," Monica answered. "It's been slow-going."

"I can always call Juniper to come down with the truck and pick him up."

"They have the wheelchair." Monica looked directly at Dutch. "It appears Homer's in the last stage of the Parkinson's."

"Seems that way. He won't go to the doctor, though."

"You know it's going to get harder and harder. Maybe you need some medical help to come here."

"He refuses everything. He wouldn't even vape for a while after all that bad press, but that turned out to be about specific pipes and what was put in them."

The trio finally arrived and Homer was short of breath, but smiling because he had managed to walk the whole way. He didn't argue, however, when it was suggested that he might sit in the wheelchair for a spell. One of the sound engineers came over to Dutch. "Hey man, things are looking good. We are just about done until the morning when we'll do the sound check with the musicians."

"That's great. Is Wavy around?" Dutch asked.

"I think he's over there talking to Tim."

Dutch walked over to that duo followed by the entourage. "Hey, Wavy and Tim, these are my friends, Jed and Monica. Jed's curator of the columbarium in San Francisco and Monica is a social worker at Glide Church."

"Curator?" Jed asked. "Haven't heard that one before. I've been called caretaker, custodian, and historian, but not curator. Isn't that for museums?"

"I've been to the columbarium," Wavy answered. "It's like a museum. Nice to meet you both." He turned to Homer. "How ya feeling today, old man?"

"Old man?" Buster interjected. "He ain't that much older than you! We're all old at this festival!"

"Hey, not everyone," Luther added. " I still have a few years left before I'm getting the senior discount." They all laughed. "And Homer walked all the way over here," Luther answered for him. Homer sighed.

"I hear you're about finished?" Dutch asked. He turned to Jed and Monica. "Tim's the sound engineer in charge. He used to work for the Grateful Dead with Owsley Stanley."

"Now him I've heard of," said Monica. "He was the one who supplied all the LSD."

"He was also their sound guy. He was my mentor," Tim replied.

"It was nice meeting you all, but I need to head back. I've got a really bad back and I can't stand so long," Wavy said. "I want to be in top form tomorrow." He got into a waiting pick-up.

"Dutch, can I talk to you?" Tim asked.

"Sure."

"I made a few calls," Tim said as they walked away. "A friend of mine is coming to the festival tomorrow and he's bringing something for Homer to try."

"I appreciate it, Tim, but I've tried a lot of different combinations of strains."

"This guy isn't a cannabis guru like you. He's a scientist who works in the Center for Psychedelic Therapies and Research. It's legit. It's part of the California Institute of Integral Studies. You've heard that there's been a resurgence of studies on the use of psychedelic drugs, haven't you?"

"I heard about it for PTSD or anxiety and depression. And addiction too, right?"

Tim nodded. "My friend and I think it has potential for Parkinson's."

"Seriously? Long term?" Dutch asked.

"We don't know. But if Homer is willing, we'd like to try. It's worked in the lab, but hasn't been tested on humans yet."

"He might be willing to be a human guinea pig. He's getting more and more depressed."

"They have been very successful using psychedelics for end-of-life anxiety when it comes to that." Dutch remained silent, so Tim quickly added, "But we don't have to bring that up if he's not ready. So maybe you and I can talk to him? Probably alone. Maybe the others with him wouldn't be on board."

"I think they'd all be on board for anything Homer wants."

"But I mean, would they try to discourage him?"

"Absolutely not. Let's have the conversation." Dutch and Tim went back to Homer's wheelchair surrounded by Luther, Buster, Jed and Monica. "Homer, Tim has something he'd like to propose."

Homer looked up at Tim who put his hand on Homer's shoulder. "There's a lot of research and studies being done on the use of psychedelics for Parkinson's."

"You talkin' about LSD?" Buster asked.

"LSD is one. Psilocybin is another. But the point is there are other plant-based therapies that are being investigated besides cannabis." Tim paused to see Homer's reaction before continuing.

Homer looked at his circle of five to gauge their reactions before answering. Not one face looked shocked or disdainful. In fact, they all looked pensive and curious. "G-g-go on," he finally said.

Tim smiled. "I have a good friend who is a research scientist at the Center for Psychedelic Therapies and Research. I've talked to him about you."

"I know the place," Monica interjected. "They've successfully treated PTSD and anxiety."

"Isn't it illegal?" Jed asked.

"The FDA has given special permission for this research," Tim answered.

"So they're experimenting with it for Parkinson's?" Monica asked.

"So far it's only been tested on animals," Tim acknowledged. He then turned toward Homer. "My friend is coming tomorrow to the festival. He's bringing some with him. Are you interested in trying? He's not a therapist, per se, but he has all the knowledge and training to assist in the procedure."

"I can be there with you, too, Homer," Monica said, taking his hand. She looked to Tim. "I'm a social worker and have some drug rehab training," she explained.

"That's perfect. What do you think, Homer?" Tim asked.

Homer turned to Dutch and looked at him inquisitively. "I think it's a good idea, Homer," Dutch replied.

"You b-b-be th-th-there too?"

"Absolutely. I'll be there with Monica," Dutch said as he patted his shoulder.

"Hey you're here!" Everyone turned to see Juniper coming down the road. She hugged Jed and Monica and then turned to Dutch. "We need to get back to the house. There are some last minute details I need you to take care of."

"Let's all go back," Dutch said. "Things are winding down here and I'm sure Jed and Monica would like to get settled in their room."

"And I need to get dinner going," Juniper said, leading the procession back to the house.

Luther trotted up to Juniper's side. "Wait'll you hear what's happening for Homer." Jed lagged behind, pushing Homer in the wheelchair while Monica talked to him about what she knew about the therapy. And Buster and Dutch brought up the rear, rehashing the final details for the festival.

29

THE EVENING DINNER WAS A HAPHAZARD EVENT. Dutch, Juniper, and Luther came and went from the table as they took care of last minute festival issues that kept popping up. Tasha and Scarlett ate quickly and went back to the animals that were freaked out over all the commotion that had disrupted their tranquil existence. Buster and Monica took over kitchen cleanup duties while Jed sat with Homer at the table. Eating remained a slow process for Homer, but his speech had improved during the day, perhaps a combination of his happiness in Jed and Monica visiting and the new blend Dutch had concocted for him.

"So you are really on board with the psychedelics?" Jed asked.

"Sure. Monica explained it to me."

"It won't hurt to try. The worst case scenario will be a bad trip for a few hours."

"You ever t-t-taken acid, Jed?"

"No. But I know plenty of people who did. I could call one of them."

"No need." Homer smiled. "I'll have Monica and Dutch with me. I'm not afraid." Jed squeezed his shoulder.

Dutch entered the room. "You need me to fill your pipe before I try to get a few hours of sleep?" Homer nodded.

"What time are people going to start arriving in the morning?" Jed asked.

"Probably five."

"I'll be up to help you."

"Thanks." Dutch turned to Homer. "I'll leave the pipe in your room." He left and Homer pushed his plate away.

"Had enough?" Jed asked. Homer nodded. "Do you want to go to bed?" Homer nodded again. Jed helped Homer into the wheelchair and pushed him out of the room.

The next morning it was still dark when Jed joined Juniper in the kitchen. "Coffee?" Juniper asked him.

"Sure."

"Do you usually get up this early?" she asked as she poured him a cup.

"I told Dutch that I wanted to help."

Juniper nodded. "There's some oatmeal on the stove if you want some."

"Thanks," Jed said before sipping his coffee. "Monica said she'd take charge of Homer for the day."

"Great. That'll give Buster time to hang with the musicians," she replied. "Dutch is already outside with Luther. I don't think either of them slept."

"Have people started arriving?"

"I think the sound guys and the caterers are starting to trickle in. Wavy's Hog Farm group has been here since four. They've done this many times and know what needs to get done." She pointed to the stove. "I'd eat something now if I were you. You don't know when you're going to eat again."

Jed scooped out some oatmeal. "Where should I go when I finish breakfast?" he asked.

"Maybe back to the sound area. Dutch is probably there waiting for Tim to show up. He was going to wait at the hotel for his friend."

"Where's Luther?"

"Helping the caterers and brewery set up."

"How about Tasha and Scarlett?"

"Feeding the animals, I guess." Juniper left and Jed quickly ate his breakfast. He went back to the room to tell Monica what was happening. She was just waking up.

"Is Homer up yet?" she asked sleepily.

"I don't think so. There's coffee and oatmeal on the stove if you want to bring some to him." He kissed her and left.

It was finally starting to get light when he got outside. He found Luther first, setting up tables. "Good morning," Luther said when he spotted Jed.

"Hey, I'm here to help. Do you need any or should I look for Dutch?"

"Probably ask him."

Jed went off to find Dutch and saw him talking to Wavy Gravy who was directing a group of people on the stage. Jed assumed they were from the Hog Farm. "Good morning," he said to Dutch and Wavy as he approached. Wavy was dressed like a clown in a tie dyed T shirt, bright yellow pants, huge clown shoes and a red derby with a red clown nose taking up half of his face.

"Hey Jed," Dutch called. He then turned to Wavy. "I'm going to leave the set-up in your capable hands and take Jed with me."

"You guys have fun!" Wavy laughed. "That's what it's all about!"

"He's quite a character," Jed said as he and Dutch walked around the farm, checking that all was going smoothly.

"One of the best. The world needs more like him."

As the sun rose higher in the sky, the guests started arriving in full force. The musicians would be arriving around eleven as the music was scheduled to start at one and they all needed to do a sound check. There were five monitors on the stage and each musician needed to inform the sound guys what mix they each wanted. Buster and Dutch greeted the musicians, while Jed became right hand man to Luther, doing whatever was needed. They finished setting up the tents for the musicians to use as dressing rooms just in time for their arrival. Buster stayed by those tents and loved being the welcoming ambassador.

First to arrive were the eldest ones. Dutch had arranged the order so that they would play first, in case they got tired and wanted to go back to the hotel. "Jed! Luther!" Buster cried out to them. "Come on over and meet Bobby Rush and Buddy Guy, both from Chicago." They shook hands. "They're gonna let me join them on stage for a couple of numbers."

"That's fantastic," Luther said. "You know my mom listened to your records a lot when I was growing up."

"I'm glad she introduced you to the blues," Buddy said. "Young people like you need to keep the blues alive."

Dutch approached the group. "Hey, the sound guys need you on stage."

"Nice meeting you," they said, following Dutch to the stage.

Other musicians started arriving with their entourages and Buster made sure to introduce them to Jed and Luther. "What a line up Dutch has for this festival!" Jed said to Luther after meeting Ry Cooder, Elvin Bishop and Charlie Musslewhite.

"And these aren't even the headliners," Luther added. "Still got Keb Mo', Robert Cray and Taj Mahal."

"Monica's most excited about seeing Bonnie Raitt," Jed grinned. "One of her favorites."

"Yeah, I've never seen Juniper so giddy either as when she talks about Bonnie Raitt."

At that moment the rest of the musicians started arriving. Jed called Monica and Luther called Juniper to tell them to come down to the dressing room tents to meet the stars. Tasha and Scarlett ran over to join them.

A little after one, Wavy went onstage and faced the crowd sprawled over the meadow. The weather was perfect and the energy joyful. He introduced some members of the Bull Creek Fire Animal Rescue, as well as some local aid groups, all of which would be recipients of the gate proceeds. Some of the money was also earmarked for Cal-Fire to use for future firefighting. Wavy did his shtick that included some of the children of the fire survivors doing circus acts. The kids did a great job of further warming up the crowd.

"And now, may I present Bobby Rush who has released another album called *Sitting On Top Of The Blues* at the ripe young age of eighty-six. His album as well as merchandise from all the performers here today, is available to buy next to the concession stands. Bobby is going to start off his set with his Grammy winner 'Porcupine Meat'."

Wavy came back onstage after Bobby had played a few songs. "Now we have the man who needs no introduction: the King of Chicago Blues, the one and only Mr. Buddy Guy!"

After Buddy finished a couple of numbers, he called Buster and Bobby Rush up and the three of them played "Sweet Home Chicago" and "Hoochie Coochie Man."

"Look at how happy Buster is playing with them!" Homer beamed.

"I'm glad he got a chance to be onstage again," Juniper replied.

Wavy came back up to introduce the next act. "Taj Mahal and Keb Mo released an album a few years ago called *Tajmo*. Can you believe we get to relish these two Blues greats together? What a treat!" They started the set with "Diving Duck Blues." They were both old friends of Dutch and they asked him to come on stage and jam with them. When he got on stage Dutch took the microphone. "I'd like to dedicate this next song, written by Keb, to a very special man in the audience, my dear friend Homer." He nodded to Buster and he and Keb started playing "Lullaby Baby Blue."

Jed nudged Monica and nodded towards Homer wiping a tear. Luther noticed their questioning look and whispered to them, "Buster played this for Homer when we were fixing up the barn."

"The next two are Hall of Fame inductees, Charlie Musselwhite into the Blues Hall of Fame and Elvin Bishop into the Rock and Roll Hall of Fame," Wavy said as the two musicians came up on the stage. "They've been touring together the last couple of years and lucky for us, they made time in their schedule for us."

Dutch had asked Wavy if he could introduce Ry Cooder. Ry had played the guitar parts for the movie *Crossroads* based on Robert Johnson. Dutch didn't mention, of course, that he owned Johnson's guitar, but he wanted to tell the Robert Johnson story of meeting the devil at the crossroads. He alluded to the fact that he had been inspired by Johnson and had met Ike Zimmerman, Johnson's mentor. "If you don't mind, Dutch, I'd like to ask Robert Cray to join us." Dutch, Robert and Ry did an incredible rendition of that famous song, "Crossroads."

"Hey, would you mind doing a couple more Robert Johnson songs?" Dutch asked the two as he left the stage. Robert and Ry whispered together and then told the session musicians backing them up what they had decided.

"Did you all know that Robert Johnson was another member of the twenty-seven club?" Ry said before they started to play.

"What does he mean by that?" Luther asked Juniper.

"A number of famous musicians died at the age of twenty-seven," she answered.

"Like who?"

"Jimi Hendrix, Janis Joplin, Kurt Cobain, Brian Jones, Jim Morrison, Amy Winehouse."

"You're kidding! How weird!"

Ry and Robert played "Me and the Devil" and then "Come on in my Kitchen."

Then it was time for Bonnie Raitt. Wavy came onstage with Bonnie and the crowd roared. "I guess I don't need to introduce this incredible lady!" Wavy laughed. "Not only is Bonnie a magnificent guitarist and singer and just about the best friend you could ever ask for, she is also asocial activist for many different causes but especially environmental ones."

"Thank you Wavy, but no one can come close to doing as much good as you do!" She kissed his cheek and turned to the crowd. "So what do you want to hear today?"

The crowd shouted back so many different songs that she ended up playing far longer than she had expected. After finishing a medley of "Angel from Montgomery," "Nick of Time," "Something to Talk About," and "I Will Not be Broken," Keb joined Bonnie to play a song they had done together for years, "No Getting over You." The music went on until nine and they ended the show with every musician backing up Bonnie doing "Love Has No Pride" and everyone together doing Wavy's signature song, "Basic Human Needs."

30

EVERYONE SLEPT IN THE NEXT MORNING, BUT EVENTUALLY THE KITCHEN FILLED WITH BLEARY-EYED FOLK BUMPING INTO ONE ANOTHER IN THEIR SEARCH FOR COFFEE. There was still a lot of cleaning up to do on the farm, but the crowd had been reminded to be ecofriendly and had not left too much in the way of paper and plastic scattered on the grounds. Homer was back in his wheelchair, the effort of the previous day causing him to regress back to an unsteady gait and shaky hands. He refused to let anyone feed him, although he was bombarded with requests. Consequently, most of his food and drink landed in his lap. The conversation among the others, however, gushed with a bubbly enthusiasm.

"Tim and his friend will be here around noon, Homer," Dutch said as he caught Monica's eye. "Best not to vape before that." Homer nodded and Monica held his trembling hand.

Luther, Jed, Dutch, Juniper, Tasha and Scarlett went outside to work, while Buster and Monica stayed in to clean up the kitchen and be with Homer whose demeanor was getting worse as the morning wore on. He shook uncontrollably, stuttering and slurring his words, and grew morose. Buster played his guitar, a feeble attempt to lighten the mood and hoping that music would once again help Homer's symptoms. But it did neither. "Where do you want to do this?" Monica asked. "In your room? The living room?"

Homer shrugged. "You d-d-d-decide."

"It's probably best for Tim's friend to decide," she replied, still holding his hand. They listened to Buster play and waited in silence.

Dutch entered the kitchen at noon with Tim and another man. "This is Calvin," Dutch said.

Calvin sat at the table and watched Homer's twitching without saying a word. The rest of the group glanced at each other, thinking it strange that he hadn't greeted anyone. Tim picked up on their discomfort. "Calvin is making observations without undue stimuli," he practically whispered. Buster looked perplexed.

The group remained silent thereon for several minutes, Calvin observing Homer, while the rest looked on. "Okay," Calvin finally said. "Where are we doing this?"

"We thought you might give us an idea of what the best location would be," Monica replied.

Calvin nodded. "We need quiet and a minimal amount of stimulus."

"How about Homer's bedroom?" Dutch asked.

"Best to be a more neutral environment. Not an overly familiar place," Tim chimed in.

"How about the room where Jed and I are staying?" Monica said. "It's very soothing and peaceful. I can just pack up our stuff and put the suitcase away." The setting was deemed suitable and all but Buster traipsed off to Monica and Jed's room.

Dutch and Monica stayed in the background as Calvin prepared the bed. "I'll leave you in Calvin's hands," Tim said. "It's a bit crowded in here. I'll go help with the clean up outside."

"Lay down, Homer." Calvin then turned to Dutch and Monica. "Are you both okay on the floor behind me?"

"Sure," they said in unison. Dutch went out and brought back some large pillows.

"Homer, what I'm giving you will make you hallucinate very little. I'm not giving you a large dose. But I need it to be big enough to see if it will work. If it helps, then you will be micro dosing every day." He turned to Dutch and

Monica. "Will you be able to give him the doses and monitor him, at least for awhile until we see how he does?"

"I can," Dutch replied. He looked at Monica. "Or Juniper and Luther."

"Tim has contacted a doctor in Mendocino who would be able to get here in a couple of hours if needed. He will know what to do if there are any problems. Tim will give you his contact info."

"Is it LSD?" Monica asked.

"No, it's called Ibogaine. It's been used successfully for drug addiction."

"Is it legal here?" she asked. "Expensive?"

"Forget the cost," Dutch said hastily. "Doesn't matter."

"Not exactly," Calvin explained. "There are treatment centers in other countries. Mexico has several. I'm allowed to use it in my research, though."

"Is it from Mexico or Central America?" Dutch asked.

"Africa." He turned to Homer. "Are you ready?"

Homer nodded. Monica slid in closer to Homer and took his trembling hand. He smiled weakly and stuttered, "N-n-not s-s-scared."

Monica squeezed his hand and smiled back. "How long does it take before it kicks in?" she asked Calvin.

"Varies with each person. Also the dosage needed varies, so it may take a little experimentation. We can only watch and wait." He turned to Homer. "It's up to you to let us know if and when you experience any change."

"K-k-kay."

"Are you going to stick around awhile?" Monica asked a bit nervously.

"I can stay until tomorrow. I want to see how he does in the first twenty-four hours before the next dose would be given." Monica nodded and glanced at Dutch who nodded back.

Meanwhile, Buster had gone back to his room. The previous day had been a busy one and he was exhausted. He was glad to be alone for a few minutes to process it. Seeing old friends and being part of the music scene again had been gratifying, but had also made him melancholy.

Later, Juniper, Luther, Tasha and Scarlett burst into the kitchen, still reeling from the exhilaration and euphoria of the festival. Jed and Tim entered after them, feeling their age as they watched their antics. Juniper opened the refrigerator and started removing vegetables and cheese. "Hey, Luther, can you get some crackers and plates? I'll make a salad," she said.

By the time they sat down at the table for lunch, the excitement had died down. Tasha was the first to bring up what was on everyone's mind. "So I wonder how Homer's doing."

"How long is it supposed to last?" Luther asked. "I mean, will he be in bed all day?"

"No, nothing like that," Tim replied. "I suspect they'll all be down later this afternoon. Calvin and I will stay in town one more night to make sure the dosage is correct. I doubt there will be a huge change after one dose, but even a small one will be better."

Dutch entered the kitchen. They all looked up at him and started talking at once. "He's doing fine," he said putting up his hand to quiet them. "I came to get some food to bring up. His speech is better, but not too much change with the tremors yet."

"Is he hallucinating?" Juniper asked.

"He says no. Calvin doesn't expect that he would because of the small dose he's getting." He turned to Luther. "Will you help me bring some food?"

Luther jumped up, happy to help. He and Dutch piled some cheese and crackers and then added some apples to the mix. "There's also some salad," Luther added.

"No, just finger food." Dutch and Luther left the kitchen and the others started talking all at once.

"So it's working?" Scarlett said.

"I don't know . . ." Juniper mused. "If the shaking is just as bad, I wonder. You know, his speech isn't so consistently bad anyway."

"It's too early to tell," Tim replied. "It's not a good idea to speculate just yet."

"Hey, where's Buster?" Tasha asked.

"Yeah, where is he?" Scarlett added.

"Probably taking a nap," Juniper said. "He did a lot yesterday." She stood. "Maybe I'll check, though." She left and they ate the rest of their meal in silence until Gypsy bounded in looking for food that had fallen on the floor.

"Oops, I forgot to feed her this morning. I wonder where Minnie is," Scarlett said putting her plate on the floor for Gypsy to eat what remained on it. She didn't have to wonder long as Minnie sauntered in, also looking for food. "Some mother I am," Scarlett muttered as she gave Minnie a piece of cheese.

"More like grandma, spoiling them like that," Juniper scoffed as she reentered the kitchen. Everyone chuckled and the mood lightened. "Buster will be down later," she said. Tim told some stories of his experiences doing sound for famous musicians and the conversation became lively once again.

After lunch, Tasha and Scarlett took the animals outside and brought Tim for a tour of the farm. Luther and Juniper were cleaning up when Buster came in. "Where's lunch?" he boomed.

"Hey old man, you slept through it!" Luther chuckled as he took a plate and piled it with some leftovers.

"How's Homer doing on that drug?" Buster asked.

"Okay, last we heard."

Buster nodded and ate silently. Luther and Juniper glanced at each other and tiptoed out of the kitchen.

31

EVERYONE CROWDED AROUND THE KITCHEN TABLE FOR A DINNER OF VEGETABLE STEW. The whole gang was there with the addition of Jed, Monica, Tim and Calvin. The Ibogaine had been a marginal success. It had definitely helped with the speech and quieted the hands enough for Homer to get food to his mouth without spilling, albeit slowly. The walking was still an issue, but he was able to use his walker, happy to leave the wheelchair in his room. Calvin and Tim had decided to keep the microdose as it was. Homer had not had any bad side effects from the drug, and they were hopeful that the walking and trembling would keep getting better with time. Dutch and Monica were more exhausted than Homer from sitting idly for all those hours. After the initial excitement over the apparent success of the treatment, they had fallen largely silent. They had both hoped for a more dramatic change, but didn't want to let on their disappointment to the others.

"Buster, would you come with me to the music room?" Dutch asked after they had finished dinner.

"Yeah, I figured we had some work to do with the gate receipts."

Dutch just nodded as he brought his dish to the sink and left the kitchen. Buster glanced at Juniper and shrugged, then did the same. "Luther and I will take care of cleaning up. You guys can go in the living room if you want," Juniper said.

"Calvin and I are going to go back to the Benbow Inn. We'll be back in the morning for the second dose and then we'll be leaving after that," Tim said.

"C'mon Homer," Jed said, helping him up. "You and I have some catching up to do. Monica, do you want to come or go rest?"

Monica smiled appreciatively at Jed for understanding her. "Rest, thanks."

"And we have animals to feed," Tasha said as she and Scarlet scurried out.

Buster sat down with Dutch in the music room. "So let's get to work and count," Buster said, rubbing his hands together.

"Actually, that's not why I asked you to come in here."

Buster looked at him curiously. "Okay."

Dutch cleared his throat and went to the closet where Robert Johnson's guitar was kept. He put in the code, opened the door and then the next door and brought it out. He handed it to Buster. "Tune it for me, will you?"

Buster tuned it as best he could. It was so old that the strings were brittle and couldn't hold the notes well. He strummed it and then started playing and singing "Crossroads" before setting it down. "So what's the point? You deciding to donate it now?"

"First the fire . . . then Homer . . . life is precious and there aren't any guarantees. Got me thinking. It's not doing any good sitting in a closet. At first I didn't want to be around when the truth came out . . . that I had the elusive Robert Johnson guitar. The mystique around the story was cool. I feel different now. I wanted your opinion."

"I agree." Buster played a few more notes.

"Are you up for a road trip?"

"You mean taking it to Phoenix?"

Dutch nodded. "Thought you'd enjoy the museum."

"Sure. Are we capable of fending off any would-be thieves? And I can't help you with the driving."

"I can ask Luther to come along and do some of the driving, and remember, no one knows the guitar even exists. It doesn't look like it's worth anything."

"Got that right. When do you want to go?"

"After Homer is stable and things have calmed down a bit here. I've emailed the Musical Instrument Museum and told them that I have a very valuable guitar, but they want me to fill out some form. I told them I needed to talk to someone first so I'm waiting for a call. Now, let's get the gate counted and the money disbursed," Dutch said as he put the guitar back in the closet.

By the time Dutch and Buster finished the business end of the festival, the lights were out in the rest of the house, everyone having gone to bed. Dutch opened the door to Homer's room to check on him. He was sleeping soundly, but snoring so Dutch knew he was okay. "Good night my friend," he whispered. "You did good today."

The group assembled at the breakfast table the next morning. Luther had helped Homer who was still adamant that he could walk with the walker and didn't need the wheelchair. Monica and Jed announced that they would be leaving that afternoon if it was okay with Homer. He nodded and smiled.

"If all goes well after a few hours on the Ibogaine, we'll leave this afternoon as well," Ted said.

"I'm sure we can handle things here," Dutch said. "I have the name of that doctor if we need him."

"I can be reached anytime at this cell number," Calvin said, handing a business card to Dutch. "And I'll return periodically to check, if that's okay."

"Of course," Dutch replied.

"Okay then, are you ready for round two, Homer?" Calvin asked patting Homer's arm.

"You bet."

Monica and Dutch each took one of Homer's arms and the four walked out. "Mind if I tag along with you again while you take care of the animals?" Tim asked Tasha and Scarlett.

"Sure," Tasha answered and those three left as well.

Buster, Juniper and Luther stayed at the table. "Dutch told us about the road trip to Phoenix," Luther said to Buster.

"Did he say why?" countered Buster.

"He didn't elaborate much," Juniper piped in. "He just said he had to bring something there and needed help driving. Are you up for such a long trip, Buster?"

"It'll be fun."

"You seem to know something we don't," Luther smiled.

"Maybe so." Buster smiled and his eyes twinkled.

"You're not going to tell us, are you?"

"Loose lips sink ships."

Luther looked at him quizzically. "Huh?"

"Old World War Two saying." Buster shook his head. "You young'uns ought to learn some history."

Homer did well on the Ibogaine and although the walking was still rough, the shaking hands seemed to be a tad better than the previous day. He decided to stay on the bed, though. He wanted to test Calvin's hypothesis that maybe for the first few days, he should rest more. "I'll be fine," Homer said to his team. "You don't need to stay here with me."

"Someone does need to be with you, Homer. We'll take turns," Dutch replied, turning to Monica. "There are enough of us here so you and Jed can get on the road."

"Let me get Jed," she answered.

"Okay Homer," Calvin said. "Dutch has the drug and the information if anything happens." He turned to Dutch. "I do want you to fill me in every day about how it's working. We may need to adjust the dosage, so it's important to keep track carefully."

"We will," Dutch replied.

"Okay, then we'll be on our way." Calvin left just as Monica returned with Jed.

"Hey, I understand you want to get rid of us," Jed teased Homer.

"You know that ain't true."

Jed smiled and hugged Homer. "You better keep in touch, old man. It was wonderful to see you."

Monica took Jed's place and held Homer's hand as she gazed into his eyes. "We'll be back soon."

Homer gazed back at her and both teared up, knowing full well that it might be the last time they see each other. He opened his mouth to speak, but shut it and nodded. They hugged and Jed and Monica left the room, both wiping tears off their cheeks. Dutch tried to decide if it was best to sit in silence and let Homer ponder things, but then decided to tell him about the guitar as a way to get his mind off it.

An hour or so later, Juniper knocked softly and opened the door. "Monica filled us in. I thought I'd relieve you a spell."

Dutch stood and winked at Homer. "Remember, mum's the word."

"What's going on?" Juniper asked. "How come you're keeping me in the dark?"

"I'll talk to you and Luther later."

Buster relieved Juniper so she could make dinner. "Dutch told me about the guitar," Homer said.

"Did you know the Robert Johnson story?" Buster asked.

"You mean how he was a shitty guitarist until he went to the crossroads and met the devil?"

"Yeah. That one."

Homer chuckled. "And then all of a sudden he was one of the best blues guitarists at that time?"

"He played rhythm, bass and slide all at the same time," Buster mused. "All on that ugly guitar."

"Wish I could come with you on that trip to Phoenix," Homer said wistfully.

"Maybe you could."

"I don't think so. This stuff is working great on my speech, but I'm not so sure about my body. I'm real tired."

Buster patted his arm. "Should I get my guitar?"

"That would be real nice." Buster got his guitar and played softly until Homer fell asleep.

Homer did make it to the kitchen for dinner, but ate little and then wanted to go back to his room. Luther got up to help him, but Dutch said, "Hey Tasha and Scarlett, would you mind helping Homer? I'd like to talk to Juniper and Luther."

They stood up and took Homer's arms. "I wanted to talk to you anyway about the summer garden," Tasha said.

"Can I stay?" Buster asked.

"Of course." And Dutch proceeded to tell Luther and Juniper the story of Robert Johnson's guitar and how he got it.

"Jeez! Crazy!" Luther said.

"You've had it here all this time?" Juniper asked.

"In that closet in my music room."

"How much do you think it's worth?" Juniper asked.

"I had it appraised – over a million, they thought. But the fact that no one knows it exists is what makes it truly priceless."

"You must have been scared shitless when the fire hit."

"I took it with me."

"Where did you go with something so valuable?" Luther asked.

Dutch smiled. "Best place I could think of. Alderpoint."

"You told them about the guitar?" Juniper asked incredulously.

"No. But I felt like that was the safest place to be with it."

"Are you going to sell it?" Luther asked.

"I don't need the money. I'd rather donate it to the Musical Instrument Museum."

Juniper and Luther both nodded. "Yeah, that's better," Luther replied.

"When will you go?" Juniper asked.

"As soon as Homer's stronger and we're sure he'll be okay."

"We can handle things here just fine," Juniper answered defensively.

"I know that. I'd just feel better if I waited until he's been on the Ibogaine longer. I'm not questioning your ability to take care of the farm or him."

"Sorry. I'm tired. It's been a hectic few days."

Luther put his arm around her and Dutch nodded. "For all of us."

A few days later things had returned to normal at the Last Resort. Homer had tolerated the dosage well and there was slow but continuous improvement in the symptoms. Dutch had spoken to a representative from the museum who had been ecstatic over the acquisition of the guitar. She and Dutch agreed to keep it a total secret so they could announce it to the media with a big blitz of publicity. "Are you going to be there when they unveil it at the museum?" Tasha asked.

"They want me to. What do you think guys?" Dutch asked Buster and Luther.

"Why not?" Buster answered. "Ain't been to Phoenix in many moons."

"Sure. It'll be fun," Luther answered, although not as wholeheartedly as Buster. He was not one who wanted to be in the spotlight.

Gordon had been pestering him about that for a while. The Innocence Project wanted to tout his success story.

Juniper picked up on his reluctance. "They don't have to know your story, Luther. I'm sure the Musical Instrument Museum is way more interested in Dutch's and Buster's stories."

"I don't think our stories are what interests them at all. It's finding Robert Johnson's guitar and knowing the real story behind its disappearance," Dutch said.

"Yeah," Buster agreed. "We're just a bunch of ordinary people trying to live our lives the best way we can. We got lucky finding this place." He looked around the table at his housemates and smiled. "We all got a second chance."

www.ingramcontent.com/pod-product-compliance
Lightning Source LLC
Chambersburg PA
CBHW051638180726
48284CB00006B/1771